Though KOOS KOMBUIS is a rock star, and a very good one at that, he has always cherished a dream of pursuing a quieter and more dignified career, such as that of an author or a bank teller. Unfortunately the banks where he applied didn't want him, and none of the numerous books he wrote in his youth received the kind of accolade he envisaged.

His first manuscript, which he produced at the age of four, went completely unnoticed. Disillusioned, he took a year's sabbatical from kindergarten to write full-time, and finished his second novel – about space-age cowboys in a far-off galaxy – before entering primary school. Little did he know that he would only start publishing in his mid-twenties! And even then, his writing career failed to take off properly. His first books, which were all published in Afrikaans, received critical acclaim but did not sell many copies.

It was only when he started performing protest music against the National Party that folk sat up and took notice. During the eighties he was banned from performing on several university campuses. The publicity generated by this official opposition led to fame, fortune, and, eventually, to the fall of the old South African government (though of course Nelson Mandela and the ANC might also have contributed their little bit).

Today, Koos is generally regarded as one of the people who has changed the cultural landscape of South Africa. Living in semi-retirement in Somerset West with his wife, two children and his laptop computer, he has once more focused his attention on writing. His autobiography, *Seks, Drugs en Boeremusiek* was reprinted many times and received only one-and-a-half negative reviews.

The
Secret Diary
of God

The Secret Diary of God

(aged 9½ million trillion years)

discovered and edited by

KOOS KOMBUIS

Published by Zebra Press
an imprint of Struik Publishers
(a division of New Holland Publishing (South Africa) (Pty) Ltd)
PO Box 1144, Cape Town, 8000
New Holland Publishing is a member of Johnnic Publishing Ltd

First published 2003

1 3 5 7 9 10 8 6 4 2

PUBLISHING MANAGER: Marlene Fryer
MANAGING EDITOR: Robert Plummer
TEXT DESIGNER: Natascha Adendorff
TYPESETTER: Natascha Adendorff

Set in 11 pt on 14.5 pt Minion

Reproduction by Hirt & Carter (Cape) (Pty) Ltd
Printed and bound by Robprint

ISBN 1 86872 671 1

www.zebrapress.co.za

Log on to our photographic website www.imagesofafrica.co.za for an African experience

Dedicated to the memory of
JOHANNES KERKORREL

"Keep on rocking in the free world!"

Contents

Thank You

To the fantasy author Robin Hobb, who encouraged me not
to be afraid to publish a book completely different
from anything I have ever written before;

To my fellow traveller, One-Love;

To Jan Ram, for showing me the stars;

To a certain person known only as "Toffie";

To my wife (some people are born perfect);

To my pop singer friends, Stef Bos and Frank Boeijen,
for brainstorming the title with me;

To my publisher, Marlene Fryer, my editor, Robert Plummer,
and the people at Zebra Press, who took an interest in me
in spite of my reputation;

To Joe Dog and Konradski for the brilliant cover design;

To Darrel Bristow-Bovey, my greatest living role model
(besides Douglas Adams, who, of course, is dead);

To Abie and Lize of Gatskop Promotions, for all
the advice on travel and gardening;

To Wynand, who once wrote me a beautiful letter in pencil by
the light of a paraffin lamp in his beach house in Nature's Valley
(I have never forgotten that letter, Wynand!);

And to God, for not striking me down in the course
of working on this manuscript.[†]

† Though I was severely persecuted by a number of insurance companies.

Foreword

Wᴀs sixteen, somebody stole my personal diary and circulated it through the town where I lived. It was a formative experience. In fact, that incident was one of the single most formative experiences of my life. It was the moment I started doubting the existence of God. It was the moment during which I understood the cruel and random hand of Fate. I seriously considered killing myself that year.

And I wasn't the only one. Numerous of my young lady friends also seriously considered killing me, having discovered, first-hand, what I really thought of them.

It is one of life's most incredible ironies that, years later, I would be the one to stumble across God's Secret Diary.

God's Secret Diary! Yes, can you believe it! And I bet there are some of you who didn't even know He kept a Diary, never mind a Secret one!

These pages were never intended for human consumption; they were meant for God's eyes only. The repercussions of this information becoming public, through an act of immense bravery on the part of my publishers, will be immense. I can only imagine the meetings going on in Heaven right now; all the frantic talk of "crisis management" and "damage control", not to mention "divine retribution". Fortunately, God is a God of love. I am quite convinced He will survive this scandal. He has survived all His previous scandals: all the noise complaints following The Big Bang, the negative reception of the basic dinosaur design which forced Him to destroy them all and find a new dominant species, Noah's drinking problem, the Jews getting lost for such an extraordinarily long time in such a small desert, Samson's bad haircut, all those embarrassing letters by St Paul, the tragic break-up of the Beatles, and all the others.

All these disasters of creation and history, and many more, are described in this Book. What makes this Book different from the Bible, though, is the fact that here we have God's own private thoughts on each and every matter *as they occurred* (or will occur). No Heavenly editor has marred these pages with politically correct dogma. Nothing has been covered up. This is the unofficial, unadulterated truth, the way things went down Behind the Scenes, the intimate thoughts and deeds of the most powerful, most lonely, most vulnerable Being ever to exist. This is the Secret Diary of God.

Before I continue, it has occurred to me that some of you may be curious as to how I located this rarest of all literary treasures. Surely God would not have left such a Book lying around for just anyone to pick up! Well, how can I put it? I suppose I could try to take you for a ride and tell you that I channelled it by means of automatic writing while in deep meditation, or that I received it on CD-ROM during my last alien abduction. The truth is far simpler than that. In actual fact, I was very lucky. At the risk of digressing somewhat, I will briefly describe the chain of events that led me to this discovery! Bear with me while I tell you a bit more about myself!

As some of you might know, I am a rock singer by profession (not a chef or a dishwasher as my name might imply). Like most other rock singers, I have spent years doing terrible things to my body and mind. Things that involved the use and abuse of countless illegal substances. I am deeply ashamed of all that now, not only the illegal substances, but also the terrible music I performed in thousands of venues across my country and elsewhere in the world. It is absolutely incredible that I have become relatively well off writing songs such as these. It is unbelievable, given the amount of illegal substances I consumed over the years, that I managed to write any songs at all.

When rock singers approach a certain crucial age, they face certain life-or-death choices. I won't reveal that age to you here. It is a trade secret. But take my word for it that all rock singers dread this age. I have seen it time and time again. When they reach this age, they can, if they really want to, carry on pretending to live as they have been living all along. This is the first option. It is not a very good option. You either end up dead or appearing to be dead. The tragic and sad careers of the members of Foreigner, the Rolling Stones and Aerosmith (especially Aerosmith) are ample proof that this is an unwise option to take. The second option is to settle down, get married, and do an occasional well-publicized show with the London Symphony Orchestra. This is known in our trade as "the Paul McCartney option". It is a safer choice, but it involves a certain loss of street credibility. And, since street credibility is more important to rock musicians than money, most rock singers deplore going down this road. So did I.

The third option for rock stars facing old age is to become writers. Since almost all rock stars are illiterate, this option is seldom taken. As far as I know, only Nick Cave, Robin Auld, Paulo Coelho and Kinky Friedman have managed to do it successfully. (Of course, Bob Dylan and John Lennon have also tried to write books, if you can call publications like *Tarantula* and *A Spaniard in the Works* books.) In any event, those precious few rock stars who turn to writing successful books are happier people than rock stars who just let themselves slide into oblivion, death or denial. They generally have a longer shelf life. After a while, they even regain the use of parts of their brains (not to mention their ears, noses, livers and lungs). Their fans are mostly intelligent people who follow their heroes' new careers with a sense of intrigue and surprise. This is all very good for business, and it also ensures that those old albums keep on selling!

Upon reaching the crucial age, and upon finally (after much soul-searching) deciding to become a writer, I eventually also had to face the logical next question: *What shall I write about?*

The answer to this question miraculously came to me one day, about a year or two ago, when I just happened to pick up the literary supplement to a well-known newspaper and perused the lists of worldwide best-selling books (both fiction and non-fiction). I couldn't help noticing how many books there were with the name "God" in the title.

As I wandered through bookstores, looking for ideas and trying hard not to think about marijuana, it struck me just how *huge* this God thing had become. God is a Big Business nowadays, almost as big a business as in the time when the Roman Empire first embraced Christianity and decided to stop feeding Christians to the lions. I noticed that, while churches (especially traditional churches) face declining membership, people from all walks of life are trying out all sorts of New Age theories. Obviously, there is a spiritual vacuum in the heart of modern man.

While perusing all this literature (and trying not to think of marijuana), I realized the inevitable: that there was a spiritual vacuum in my own heart, too. I started wondering whether God would reveal

Himself to me if I asked Him nicely. Or if I at least attempted to reach some higher spiritual plane (without the aid of marijuana, of course).

I tried out various forms of meditation. I drank a lot of green tea (the stuff you buy in Woolworths, not the stuff you pick up at your dealer). I even tried my hand at gardening (all the while keeping my eyes open for encrypted stones and ancient papyrus manuscripts).

Alas, all to no avail.

Then, round about six months ago (the synchronicity of all this was simply amazing), I came across a book called *The Bible Code*. It struck me as a particularly clever book (though, quite obviously, a hoax), and I started visiting websites on the Internet that explained the phenomenon described in it.

It did not take me long to write my own computer program, copying the one used by Mr Drosnin and his friends. My reason for doing so was more cynical than anything else, although a part of me wanted to believe that there might just be a grain of truth in all this!

Yet I couldn't help thinking: even if this theory *was* true, and God would bother contacting mankind using an IQ test such as this one, surely He would go all the way? He would make it *really* difficult. He wouldn't leave His message lying around in such an obvious book as the Bible. He would hide it carefully in the most insignificant, most ignored, most boring literary work of all time.

In the course of time I ran several such boring, insignificant pieces of text through my computer, but I found nothing but gibberish or incidental and random patterns. I tried my program on books like *Henry VIII* (Shakespeare's worst play), *Paradise Regained* by John Milton (the first example of a sequel being vastly inferior to the original), *From Yalta to Vietnam* by Dave Horowitz (a book explaining why Communist Russia would outlast capitalist America), Andy Warhol's posthumous diaries, *The Sex Life of F.R. Leavis – A Short Biography* by Mary-Anne Hawthorp, *The Complete Lyrics of John Denver* (by John Denver, of course), *For the Record* (the forgotten autobiography of Gary Teichmann), *Ulysses* by James Joyce, and *P is for Peril* by Sue Grafton. Of all these books, only *Ulysses* by James Joyce yielded an interesting result; when I applied my program to this monumental tome, out popped the exact, complete script of *Finnegan's Wake*, James Joyce's next book. This, of course, did not prove the existence of God. If it proved anything at all, it merely confirmed what everyone knew anyway: that James Joyce was a complete lunatic, definitely Irish, and decades ahead of (or behind) his time.

I was about to give up when, on a hunch, I tried the program on a book I found in a friend's attic. It was dirty, tattered and torn, and almost as fragile with age as the Dead Sea Scrolls. It was – believe it or not – the telephone directory for Potchefstroom from the year 1964. (For those of you who don't know, Potchefstroom is an insignificant, though rather pretty little village in South Africa.) After all those miserable failures, I struck gold on this one. In a big way.

The 1964 Potchefstroom telephone directory revealed not one, but several hidden manuscripts, all in perfectly understandable English. The first one I found, using the most direct horizontal grid method, was called *The Secret Diary of God (aged 9½ million trillion years)*. At first I thought this was a joke, of course, but in spite of myself, I started wondering whether this was the real thing, and whether God was trying to tell the world that He actually had a sense of humour and a talent for satire.

More surprises followed! A second manuscript emerged when I applied the vertical grid method – it appears to be a kind of sequel, based on the "Harry Potter" success formula, written by a friend of God (guess what his name was?). And even *more* manuscripts became evident when I switched the numerical value of the telephone numbers with letters of the alphabet! Of these, by far the most interesting is a lengthy treatise on famous and influential people who originated from Potchefstroom. It contains biographies of, among others, F.W. de Klerk, Rina Hugo, Albert du Plessis and Pieter van Zyl (the fat guy who tackled the rugby ref), and is entitled *The Potchefstroom Book of the Dead*. Working backwards, the telephone directory contains various works of fiction, numerous apocryphal gospels (including a very lewd one by Mary Magdalen), and at least one collection of recipes.

Unbelievable, eh? What a find! What an extraordinary piece of good luck!

I have decided to publish only God's Diary at this point.

I am keeping the other manuscripts safely at home, such as the recipes, *The Gospel According to Mary Magdalen* and *The First and Second Holy Books of Harry* (much of this is downright offensive; I am holding back that material for a follow-up publication later on).

Discovering these hidden codes inside the 1964 Potchefstroom telephone directory has not only changed my own life (I am now a firm believer in God), but it is bound to change the lives of many people who read this book. The Post Office of Potchefstroom has assured me that no other copies of the 1964 telephone directory still exist; and, according to the best legal minds I have consulted, no one has ever claimed royalties or authorship for a telephone directory. Which means, to put it bluntly, that I, and I alone, will get rich from this publication (and all other publications that might follow it).

Not only will I get rich, I will become famous, too. I might be invited to meet Oprah! I will rub shoulders with Deepak Chopra and Gary Zukav at luncheons! I will be remembered long after the Dalai Lama has passed on (although, of course, he will come back in another incarnation). If things really go according to plan, some guys – probably a bunch of crazy Americans – will get together and start a new church with this book as its Bible. (I hope they don't kill themselves in the end, but even if they do, you can't complain about that kind of publicity.)

After all, I deserve some remuneration. I suffered for this truth! I deciphered this book under unbelievably difficult circumstances (I am a rock star, remember?). During the entire process my cellphone rang constantly, I was still receiving e-mails by the truck-load, and I was harassed at my front door by the press, by groupies wanting my autograph, by agents wanting to book me for album deals and tours. It was extremely painful, I tell you.

Not only was it painful to publish a book under such circumstances; it was downright heartbreaking. The final chapters, especially, made me tremble with sorrow. Is this really what our world is coming to? Is it the final fate of all civilizations on Planet Earth to come to such a disgraceful end? Will God never regain His sense of humour? If the inevitability of this scenario is too much to bear for some sensitive souls, I am truly sorry. However, there is nothing I can do about it. I am merely a humble vessel.

Thank you very much for believing this unbelievably tall story (I wouldn't have!) and buying this book.

Yours irreverently,
KOOS KOMBUIS

We are condemned to freedom.

— JEAN-PAUL SARTRE

Part One

THE
EARLY
YEARS

1
Designing the Universe

VERSE ONE
In the beginning I had no idea what I was doing.

VERSE TWO
I was all alone, then – Heaven was much smaller, the basement had not yet been added, and I had no company whatsoever.

VERSE THREE
Not even angels! No kitchen staff! No Board of Directors! No prayers to answer, no consultants, no one to bother Me with meddlesome questions such as: "How many angels can dance on a pinhead?" or "Why do bad things happen to good people?" or "Where do ants go on holiday?"

VERSE FOUR
Oh, what bliss it was back then!

VERSE FIVE
Yet, to be quite honest, there were times when I felt rather lonely ...

VERSE SIX
I remember waking up one morning and saying to Myself: Let's create a Universe. Let's create a Universe, and fill it with all sorts of life forms: Amoebae! Fish! Spiders! Little crawly slimy things! Maybe an elephant or two!

VERSE SEVEN
This was easier said than done, as you can imagine (a Universe is a very large thing to make). I had to try quite a few times before I got the general structure right.

VERSE EIGHT
And, of course, when You make something as large as a Universe, You can do with a few extra hands. I had no choice but to create a multitude of angels first. I needed them to run errands while I worked at My computer and pored over complicated long-division sums.

VERSE NINE
The angels! Oh, how I wish I had never bothered with them. They were a dreadful bore. They were so grateful I had made them that they kept on thanking and praising Me, and playing irritating screechy little songs on their little harps.

VERSE TEN
They were almost completely useless, and they had no sense of humour, no grasp of irony. To be honest, they were awful company.

VERSE ELEVEN
Moreover, their presence was such a distraction that I kept on making elementary mistakes. My first couple of Universes were disastrous!

VERSE ... Oh, damn these verses anyway. It's not as if I'm ever going to publish any of this!

What was I saying? Oh, yes, the first Universe failed to expand, and fell back into itself immediately. The second expanded into infinity and eventually evaporated. The third one had a fine shape, but I had forgotten to add water, so nothing could live in it. The fourth one had water, and it had a stable form, yet nothing happened. The fifth one ... Oh, never mind the details! Suffice it to say that there were about twenty attempts before I finally worked out the basic design.

One thing all these failed Universes had lacked was the shape of a spiral. If you don't believe Me, try this at home! Try creating life with linear DNA! Try to make a beach look pretty with rectangular shells! Try to spin a cube-shaped galaxy into vacant space! It simply doesn't work.

So it was back to the drawing board. I tore up all My previous notes, diagrams and calculations, and started anew.

At this point, the angels were getting bored, and they asked Me to create some more of them as they needed a horn section for their band. I could see no harm in that – I reckoned, anything to keep them busy – so I obliged. I spent a bit of extra time on one angel, whom I called Lucifer – quite a pretty angel – and appointed him leader of the horn section. I must say, I liked Lucifer right away. He didn't waste time praising Me for creating him, but started doing his job immediately. The new horn section made a terrible racket, but at least now they were also doing secular stuff, even a bit of rhythm 'n blues, and they weren't so much under My feet any more.

What I really wanted to do was create a Universe that was somehow alive, a Universe that could look after itself once it had been triggered into action. A place that did not require constant meddling and supervision. A self-catering Universe, in other words.

Using the shape of a spiral, I managed to curl all the raw material needed for this Universe into a tiny ball. The concept was elegant yet simple: imagine a spiral staircase going, not up, but down, for all eternity! Imagine folding, and refolding, the same slip of paper until nothing remains. Once detonated, this process is reversed, and the spiral staircase bounces upward, and out. The actual explosion caused by such a drastic reversal of energy would, of course, be enormous. I knew that it was bound to disrupt Lucifer's band practice, but decided not to warn them. I wanted the whole thing to be a surprise. I wanted the angels to stop treating Me with such awe and show a bit of scientific interest. I had worked so hard and for so long that I felt I needed a pat on the back.

What I got was more like a stab in the back than a pat on the back ...

2
The
Big Bang,
etc.

Dᴇᴀʀ ᴅɪᴀʀʏ (you don't mind if I call you that, do you?),

It is only a couple of aeons since My last entry, and already everything has taken a turn for the worse.

I feel as if I have lost control. Heaven is no longer the peaceful place it used to be. And this blasted Universe is taking longer to develop than I intended.

At first, everything seemed to go very well. The Big Bang was everything I had expected it to be. When the fateful day dawned, the final Universe cracked open like a gigantic bottle of champagne. The noise was earth-shattering! Bits and pieces flew everywhere! The angels complained! Lucifer wouldn't speak to Me for months! Heaven was filled with smoke and debris!

I could tell right away that, at last, I had achieved success. As time passed, stars lit up the firmament one by one. Galaxies unfurled themselves gracefully and stretched their bejewelled spiral tentacles through the void. And, oh, the little planets, the planets that formed from the dust of the explosion were the cutest tiny things. Some were covered with ammonia, others with water, some were made entirely of gas. Every single one had the potential, however remote, for life.

I got up every day and went to My bay windows to see how the Universe was doing, and look at all the new constellations that had formed overnight. And I waited. I waited for the miracle that was to come at the end. The miracle I had yet told no one about. The surprise I had hidden right at the bottom of the eternal spiral staircase of causality.

The creation, at last, of a creature far more intelligent and interesting than the angels.

But up till now, that has not yet happened.

Technically, I can see nothing wrong with the Universe. All the laws of physics I had programmed into it work very well. Gravity is everywhere, and the suns burst into flames and sizzle out exactly as planned. The black holes take care of the refuse by sucking all the failed planets and unwanted stuff into another dimension.

What bothers Me is that, though there are vast numbers of planets able to sustain life, and though a sizeable number of life forms have emerged, there is absolutely no sign so far of intelligent life.

On lots of planets, and in many star systems, many different thingies have started oozing from the primordial mud and dust and slimy gloop. On some planets, dominant life forms have begun to assert themselves. There are planets ruled by jellyfish, there are planets ruled by snails, and there are planets ruled by insects. There is even one planet ruled by large lizard-like creatures called dinosaurs. These dinosaurs are extremely clumsy and uncouth, and they do a lot of damage, not only to one another – most of them are flesh-eating – but to all the natural fauna and flora of their planet. They run through the foliage! They trample the flowers! They leave nasty big droppings everywhere!

It would not have bothered Me all that much if not for the fact that the planet where these beasts reside is, so far, the planet with the most promising ecosystem. If intelligent life emerges one day, it will almost certainly be on this planet.

I was standing talking to Lucifer the other day,[†] watching this planet – it is called Earth – through My bay windows as it moved past.

"Just look at those ugly things," I said, pointing out the dinosaurs. "I wonder what leap of evolution gave birth to such ghastly animals?"

"Why don't You destroy them?" Lucifer asked.

I was horrified at his suggestion. "How can you even think such a thought?" I gasped. "Don't you understand that the whole point of a self-catering Universe is that there is nothing you or I can do to stop this kind of thing? I have vowed to stick to a policy of strict non-intervention."

"But You are God," Lucifer pointed out. "You can do what You like. If You give things a little shove in the right direction, surely no one would be any the wiser?"

"Mmm," I said. I had to admit, for an angel this guy had quite an original mind.

"Non-intervention is no better than voyeurism," Lucifer snarled. "What You are basically doing here is watching TV."

"Reality TV," I corrected him. "It is slightly more entertaining than regular TV."

Lucifer ignored My little joke, and pointed to another area of the sky instead. "See that big asteroid over there? As things are now, if it keeps on moving in the direction in which it is moving, it will miss Earth by a few hundred thousand miles.[‡] However, if You were to give it a little nudge in the right direction ... just a tiny little nudge ..."

---

† We were still on speaking terms then.
‡ These were the days before the metric system.

"It would hit Earth," I mused.

"Indeed. Of course, it won't destroy Earth. Nor will it destroy all life on Earth. It will just knock the dinosaurs into smithereens. There will be a slight delay of a couple of thousand Earth years, and then evolution will take its course again, and another dominant life form will emerge on that planet." He smiled at Me slyly. "Probably that special life form You had envisaged in the first place."

Of all the angels, Lucifer was the only one who, I realized then, had an inkling of the surprise I had planned. It was probably because he was the only angel showing any interest in science.

"It's a tempting scenario," I admitted. "But I'm not sure that I want to make such a decision on My own. I wish I could get a second opinion."

Lucifer laughed. "That must be the worst thing about being God, never being able to get a second opinion."

He turned away from the bay window and walked across to My liquor cabinet – yes, he walked straight towards it, as if he had done so millions of times before – where he poured Us each a stiff drink. He had a pensive expression on his angelic face.

Of course, I should have put two and two together right then. It was pretty obvious that the rascal had been going through My private notes while I was asleep! How could he otherwise have understood so much about the workings of asteroids? And how on Earth, I mean how in Heaven, did he know where My liquor cabinet was?

But when he spoke next, his voice was very sincere, though he didn't look Me in the eye. He just steered Me through the room, his right arm buddy-like across My shoulders, and spoke to Me in an intense, almost conspiratorial whisper.

"I'll tell You what, though, God. Why don't You let me select all the smartest angels I know, all the ones who have demonstrated some leadership qualities? I will get them together and they can serve as a kind of consulting body. Why don't We convene a meeting for, say, this time tomorrow, explain the whole dilemma to them, all the pros and cons, and then vote on it? That way, if they vote to destroy the dinosaurs, it won't actually be Your fault if things go wrong because of it."

Jeez, that guy had a mouth on him. The way he sometimes talked, I bet he could sell electricity to a quasar!

At first, I flatly refused even to consider Lucifer's suggestion.

But, as time went by, I found Myself wondering about it more and more.

Just one tiny little nudge ...

Hmmmm?

3

The Destruction of the Dinosaurs

AND SO IT came to pass, dear Diary, that I went along with the idea, of course. And, before I knew it, the Board of Directors was born.

I did find it a bit strange that among the angels Lucifer selected to serve on the Board of Directors was his entire horn section.

I also thought it rather odd that he'd brought along someone I had never met before, a guy called "Nietzsche", whom he introduced as his "lawyer".

"What's a lawyer?" I asked Lucifer.

"Well, You know, he's not actually going to take part in the proceedings or vote or anything. It's just that having a lawyer around makes everyone feel so much more important. Lawyers are very clever, You know. Some of them can even speak Latin."

Though I was somewhat mystified, I allowed Nietzsche to be present. He was quiet most of the time, though he took a lot of notes and often frowned. Now and then he left the room for a break and came back smelling of cigarette smoke.

Lucifer was evidently very well prepared for the meeting. Within seconds he had an overhead projector rigged up, and proceeded to present, to his captive audience, a complete slide show about the dinosaurs.

It was a hideous slide show. He had somehow ensured that the photographer had caught the dinosaurs showing all their worst angles, and doing the most beastly things. During the course of the show, several angels got sick and had to go to the bathroom. Even Lucifer himself was somewhat green in the face, and left the room with the lawyer for a smoke break at least twice. There was no doubt which way the voting would go. Everyone hated the dinosaurs.

I gave a little speech after the presentation, trying to explain My qualms about destroying this species in spite of the fact that they were so obviously repugnant. I tried to describe My original vision of a self-catering Universe. I told the angels to carefully consider both sides of the issue before casting their votes.

I ended My lecture with the statement: "Let Us not set a potentially harmful precedent, gentlemen. Let Us be careful not to throw out the baby with the bath water." I was quite pleased to see Nietzsche writing this down, but My bubble of satisfaction was immediately burst when Belial, the saxophone player in Lucifer's horn section, asked: "What's a baby?"

"Oh, never mind," I said, and sat down.

After this, Nietzsche got up and briefly spoke a few words. He told Us that the vote would be binding, and that all future decisions pertaining to the future of the Universe would be binding, and that henceforth no such decisions would be allowed to be taken without the full knowledge of all the members of the Board of Directors. Then he gave Us each a piece of paper, inscribed in Latin, which We had to sign.

"Do You agree with this stipulation, God?" he asked Me as I looked at the document.

"Well," I said, "I don't think it will be necessary to meddle any further with any species, so whether I sign or not, nothing is going to change. Destroying the dinosaurs is a one-off, I'm certain of that! After this, the Universe will be self-catering again."

"That's true, God," Lucifer said. "No further meddling. It will make no difference whether You sign or not." He was smiling brightly. Or was that a hint of a smirk? Then he winked and looked at Nietzsche. "It will make my lawyer a happier man, though. Lawyers are dreadfully unhappy when people won't sign their papers."

So I signed, and thought no more of it.

4

The Origin
of Evil

Dear diary,

I honestly believed that the Board of Directors would never need to convene again. Nor did I expect ever to meet the lawyer guy again. As it turned out, after the destruction of the dinosaurs – which, incidentally, went according to plan – the Board of Directors, for some reason or other, started convening on a weekly basis. And this Nietzsche chap was present at every single meeting, always making speeches, always saying things in Latin, and generally getting everyone all worked up about nothing at all.

Oh, the pointless decisions that were taken at these meetings! Really, I still believe to this day that none of it was necessary.

For example, a general refuse-collecting day was decided upon. From now on, black holes were only allowed to operate on Thursdays. All refuse had to be collected in black plastic bags at the entry to the black holes so that, come Thursday, it could be sucked into another dimension.

Then it was decided that there should be a general speed limit throughout the Universe. Nothing would ever be allowed to travel faster than the speed of light.

"But," I pointed out, "nothing can move faster than light anyway."

"Is that an absolute rule?" Nietzsche asked. "What I mean is, is it a law, like the laws of physics, or does light just happen to be the fastest thing around?"[†]

"I … I don't know," I admitted. "It's never bothered Me before."

That settled it, then. A general speed limit was declared, and angels were sent out to all remote corners of the Universe to put up signs forbidding anything or anybody to travel faster than the speed of light, ever.

All this red tape caused Me to sink into a profound depression. I felt futile, enraged and bored. I felt I was losing control of My own Universe. I had been upstaged and thwarted by a bunch of squeaky-voiced angels.

And if that wasn't bad enough, the other day, out of the blue, it came to My notice that, perhaps, I am not the only God around.

Up till that point I had sort of taken it for granted that I am Omnipotent, All-Powerful and Infinitely Wise. That I, and I alone, am responsible for all life, movement and activity all over the show.

Then I started hearing rumours of other Gods besides Myself. Someone – I think it was Gabriel – mentioned a Guy called Zeus. There was talk in the corridors of Heaven, snatches of conversation, hinting at Gods called Buddha, Odin, Krishna and Ra. Apparently, They all admire My work. They have no intention of challenging My authority or anything like that. But They are Gods as well. Not angels, not lawyers, not intelligent life forms springing from My Universe, but Gods.

† Clearly Nietzsche hadn't read Einstein's *General Theory of Relativity* yet. At that stage, neither had I.

It baffled Me. I had no idea where They could possibly have come from!

As if this was not enough, I found out shortly afterwards that, not only were there more Gods around besides Myself, there was also more than one lawyer in Heaven.

One day I received a call from someone who introduced himself simply as "Paul".

"Is this God I am speaking to?" he asked, after introducing himself.

"Yes, Paul, how may I help you?" I replied.

"I have heard about Your problems with Lucifer and the Board of Directors and about how they are influencing Your laissez-faire policy of running the Universe. I am here to offer my services."

"How can a guy called Paul, who I have never heard of before, help Me in any way?" I asked, almost throwing down the telephone.

"I am a lawyer," he explained. "And a very good one, too. Better than Nietzsche. I would like to represent You at the Board of Directors meetings from now on. I also have some private suggestions to make."

"Do you have any references?" I asked warily, for by now I had come to realize that lawyers simply can't be taken at face value.

"Oh, yes. I once busted Bacchus out of jail after He was caught drunk and disorderly in the Milky Way. I have also provided consultation for Ra and Zeus, and, best of all, I think I might have some dirt on Lucifer."

"You're hired," I said. "I don't care about Bacchus, Ra or Zeus, but I must admit I'm interested in ... um ... what you know about Lucifer. He's starting to irritate Me."

"Would You care to meet me and sign some papers?" he asked.

"As long as they're not in Latin," I sighed.

My first conference with Paul took place in strict secrecy. We met at night, in the parking lot behind the country club. We arrived in separate unmarked vehicles; Mine was driven by Gabriel, and I was in the back seat, wearing a false beard and a wide straw hat. Paul was already there, wearing shades and drinking mineral water. He spoke in a hushed voice. In the country club, barely a hundred yards away, the sounds of revelry could be heard. Lucifer and his friends were celebrating some new deal they had struck somewhere in the Milky Way.

"Listen, God, Lucifer is trying to take over. He wants to be God in Your place," Paul informed Me, adjusting his shades and looking this way and that.

"I have been suspecting that," I said. "I caught him out, only last week, trying to cheat at chess."

"I suggest You throw him out of Heaven," Paul hissed.

"Okay with Me," I whispered.

"There is only one problem."

"Problem? How could there possibly be a problem? I am God. I can do what I like."

"Famous last words," Paul chuckled. "Didn't Nietzsche make You sign a piece of paper?"

"Yeah, but so what?"

"Do You have a copy of it?"

"No …"

"Never mind. I've seen the original, so here's how things will be going down from now on. Technically, You can fire Lucifer and his entire horn section, but You will never be entirely rid of them. They are still to be included in all Your most important decisions. What's more, the ultimate destiny of the Universe is no longer in Your hands. It will depend on the choice of a third party."

"Who is this third party?" I asked suspiciously, thinking with some paranoia of Zeus, Buddha, Krishna and Ra.

"It will all depend on a bloke called Adam."

"Adam? Adam who?"

"You mean You haven't noticed? A new dominant species has appeared on Earth since the destruction of the dinosaurs."

I felt a chill running up and down My spine. It had been a while since I'd noticed developments on Earth. I'd been too busy writing My Diary and worrying about other Gods. Now, finally, I had been caught napping while the most important step in evolution had been going on behind My back.[†] It was most embarrassing. It was the stuff nightmares were made of, the kind of thing I had feared ever since I'd begun to lose control ...

"Adam is different from the dinosaurs in shape and personality, but should he take Lucifer's side against You, he might become equally repulsive. If not in appearance, then in habits. He will stop being a vegetarian. He will get into dirty sex. In fact, he might get into dirty sex anyway. Observers believe the only reason he hasn't turned to dirty sex up till now is the lack of a female partner."

All this was a bit much to take in all at once. I couldn't wait to get back to My own quarters, open My bay windows, and check out this creature for Myself. Yet now I had to cope with the fact that My best idea, My prize creation, may already have been hijacked by Lucifer.

Fury took hold of Me. I wanted to avenge Myself on this renegade angel. Right away. I had never ever been so angry before in My life. Ever.

As luck would have it, at that very moment the doors to the country club opened, and a bunch of drunken angels poured into the parking lot. I recognized their faces; they were the members of Lucifer's horn section – Beelzebub, Mephistopheles, Azazel, Belial, and all the others.

---

† Time on Earth, as everyone knows, moves much, much faster than time in Heaven.

Lucifer himself followed behind them, waltzing down the stairs, swinging a bottle of bourbon in his hand. He seemed strangely trans-figured, less angel-like on the one hand – his face almost resembled that of a snake, the lowest form of dinosaur, the one that never evolved limbs – yet, on the other hand, he appeared almost God-like in his wrath, almost like a mirror image of Myself ... My evil twin, so to speak.

I got out of the car, removed My straw hat, rose to My full height, and addressed Lucifer and his crew of drunken angels.

"Henceforth," I announced, "your services will no longer be required in Heaven. I will cast you out, all of you, to a basement which I shall prepare for My enemies. The basement will be called Hell, and it will be a very unpleasant place. It will be hot, and humid, and there will be no view at all. That is where you will stay, except for the times Our contractual obligations permit you to meet with Me in Our conferences as the Board of Directors."

Lucifer seemed almost pleased to see Me. He, too, rose to his full stature, and faced Me without any fear or embarrassment whatsoever; a creature of pure evil, yet not ashamed; confident in, and relaxed with his new identity.

"Our contract allows for more than that," he snarled. "As of tomorrow, I will also live on Earth. There, I will present my case to Your creature Adam. If he makes up his mind and chooses correctly, Earth will become my main sphere of influence. And all human beings who join me in my rebellion against You will help me to overthrow You in the next democratic election."

"Democratic election?" I glanced at Paul, helplessly. "What is this business about a democratic election?"

"I have been meaning to tell You, God," Paul sighed. "This was my idea, and it represents a kind of out-of-court settlement with

Nietzsche. It is the only way this battle can ever be decided. I have brought the papers with me, if You feel up to signing them ..."

"As long as they're not in Latin!" I exclaimed. "As long as it means that one day, some way, somehow, We can defeat this Lucifer, this Devil, this Satan, this rotten angel and his ... his ..."

"Devil," I heard Lucifer say to himself, almost lovingly. "Devil. I kind of like that name. Devil, Satan. Yes, why not? The time is ripe for a change of image ..."

As he left, laughing and puking and burping with his band of drunken angels, I could swear I saw real horns protruding from his forehead.

5

The Evolution of Adam

D<small>EAR DIARY</small>,

This meeting with Paul was the start of a long and rather ambiguous friendship. Since signing that piece of paper (which wasn't in Latin) agreeing to a fair and square election battle, some time in the future, between Myself and the Devil, Paul has been My right-hand man. He has advised Me, He has pondered My great decisions with Me, and he is also acting as the ghostwriter for My official autobiography.

"What do I need an autobiography for?" I couldn't help asking.

"As part of Your election campaign, of course!"

"Oh ..."

"We must, from now on, start polishing and promoting Your public image as much as We possibly can. That way, when the election date comes around, You will stand a better chance."

That, incidentally, is one of My main reasons for continuing to write this secret Diary.

However much I like Paul, I have a basic mistrust of lawyers, and I am afraid that the official version of events, when it eventually gets published, might be so far from the truth as to be totally unrecognizable.

For instance, it was Paul who suggested the idea that I should pretend, to future readers, that I created the world and all its species in seven days.

Seven days! How preposterous! How on Earth (excuse the pun) can anyone create all that in seven days! All the mountains, all the deserts, all the flowers, all the trees, the whole sea and all the fish in it, all the birds, beasts and animals, not to mention Adam!

Speaking of Adam! Ah, Adam.

How shall I describe him? He turned out to be quite a surprise.

He walks on his back feet, like some of the dinosaurs did, but without that dreadful slouch. Physically, he resembles the angels and everyone in Heaven; one can go so far as to say that he resembles Me.

I have been watching him for days now, and I must admit I am fascinated. Adam, though he looks a bit like a regular angel – minus the wings and tinted contact lenses which are the latest trend in Heaven – has a unique personality. He is neither angel nor animal. Instead of praising Me for creating him, he philosophizes about things. Instead of rushing around foraging in the forest for food, he walks around on his hind legs and looks up at the sky and the stars, and ponders the great mysteries of life.

"Who am I?" he keeps on asking. "What am I doing here?" "What is the point of living?" And sometimes: "Why aren't there any women around here?"

This last question I find a bit bothersome, of course. It is pretty obvious that, unlike most of the other species on Earth, Adam has evolved alone. He looks like a male, but no female has developed to accompany him. This lack of companionship – or, as Paul somewhat condescendingly calls it, this lack of "dirty sex" – is one of the greatest and most persistent existentialist questions on Adam's mind.

I'm not sure what to do about this problem yet. At any given moment, My other problems may start overtaking Me.

This may indeed be the calm before the storm.

So far, the situation with the Devil has reached an impasse. According to rumours, he is somewhere on Earth, where he intends to turn Adam against Me. I haven't seen him there, though. His fellow fallen angels from the horn section are down below in the basement. They constantly complain about the heat and unpleasant circumstances – I can sometimes hear their cries of agony rising up through the air vents, especially on quiet nights – but, if you can pardon the irony, their plight leaves Me cold. It was their choice to side with Lucifer. They should never have started that rhythm 'n blues stuff in the first place.

I know that I will have to face the Devil and all his angels the next time a Board of Directors meeting is convened. That problem, however, hopefully belongs to the distant future. Paul and Nietzsche have struck a deal which stipulates that Board meetings are unnecessary unless an urgent decision has to be taken.

If I were to create a female partner for Adam, for instance, or feel like meddling with anything else on Earth, I would be legally bound to call together the entire Board.

Paul himself is dead set against Me creating a woman for Adam.

"But the guy's got to procreate," I keep on telling him.

"Can't You make him clone himself?" Paul insists on asking. "Do You realize what kind of problems a female Adam might cause?"

"I can see he is lonely," I would respond. "His frantic masturbation is beginning to interfere with his existentialist musings."

Sometimes I wonder whether Paul has a problem with his feminine side. Honestly, the man is such a prude!

P.S. I am writing this postscript in the dead of night by the light of a single candle. I am going to slip down to Earth Myself and make a woman for Adam. This way, I can bypass the Board of Directors.

Technically, I won't be breaking any rules. I will not create a new being out of thin air. I intend using one or more of Adam's own body parts and just changing them a little bit.

Please don't tell anybody!! If anyone finds this Diary, please burn it! No one must ever know about it!! Especially not Paul!!! No one must ever know that I had a hand in the creation of Eve. The legal implications would be horrific. I could be sued till the end of time.

It's a dirty job, but Somebody's got to do it.

6
The Creation of Eve

P HEW! WHAT A night!

I've never worked so hard in My life before.

In fact, come to think of it, I've never done any manual labour Myself. Not ever. Last night was the first time. It felt really strange. I worked up quite a sweat, though, and when I returned to Heaven I was so tired I slept like a baby (whatever that is).

Let Me tell you, dear Diary, how it happened. Let Me give you a blow-by-blow account.

When I arrived on Earth, Adam was fast asleep. There was no one around to see what I was doing.

Halfway through the operation, unfortunately, he woke up. "Who are You?" he asked groggily.

I decided to tell him the truth. "I'm God," I said.

"God? Really? Do You actually exist?" He shook My hand, smiling profusely. "Are You the famous Dude who put all this together? I've often wondered whether it was You or not! Wow, Man! I really love Your work!"

"Er ... that's very nice, Adam, but you've got to go back to sleep now. I'm removing one of your ribs and I don't want you to be conscious. It might hurt."

He looked confused. "What would You want one of my ribs for?"

"To make a woman for you."

"Honestly! Really? I'm going to have a woman? My very own live woman?"

"Yes."

His eyes were wild with anticipation. "Look, God, do me a favour and count my ribs. Do You think that, while You're about it, You could possibly make ... er ... more than one woman? You see, I've been having these fantasies ... Tell me, how many ribs have I got? Take them all, please! What do I need ribs for if I can have ..."

"For Pete's sake, Adam, one is enough, don't you think?"

"Who's Pete?" Suddenly he looked around, horrified. "Don't tell me You're going to make more men, too!"

"No, Pete's just an expression. There isn't actually a guy called Pete. Well, not yet."

"There'd better not be." He sighed, and closed his eyes. "Okay, God, You win. One woman or many, it doesn't matter. Just hurry up. I'm going back to sleep now." There was a pleasant smile on his face. "And when I wake up I won't be lonely any more, will I?"

"No, Adam. When you wake up, you won't be lonely any more. That's a promise."

He looked so vulnerable then, so innocent in sleep, such a pure, unspoilt person, such a childlike creature of the night, that it broke My heart to carry on operating on him. I felt as if the operation was forever marring his perfect body.

Yet I need not have feared, for when I had removed the rib and closed up the wound, not even a scar remained. No evidence at all existed of My secret deed.

The rest was the hardest part. I had to dig a hole in the ground and put the rib in it. Then I had to wait for it to turn into a woman.

Sounds simple, doesn't it? Problem is, I had never dug a hole in the ground before. Not with My bare hands! It was back-breaking, difficult work. Crawling in the soil were all sorts of creeping things and slimy things. The ground got stuck under My nails. I could smell stuff rotting around Me. At one stage I imagined some kind of creature crawling or slithering past in the undergrowth and hissing at Me.

Finally, however, it was all over, the hole was deep enough, and I put Adam's rib into the ground in an upright position. Then I fashioned some loose earth around the rib roughly in the shape of a woman. I gave her some breasts – not too big or too small – and long hair, and a nice round bum. Then I altered her genetic make-up ever so slightly. She would have a marginally different personality from Adam. She would be good at cooking, and at asking directions from strangers, and finding missing things around the house.

It was dark, though, and I couldn't see very clearly what I was doing. It is possible that I might have got some of the genes wrong. In fact, now that I think of it, I'm sure I forgot to give her logical faculties. Oh, well, never mind! She will just have to depend on Adam for that. It will force them to stay together ... he will need her for her sensual appeal and practical skills, and she will need him whenever she encounters a problem that requires any form of rational thought.

Then I washed My hands in a stream and left. The woman would be ready by morning. Adam would be ecstatic.

I haven't actually looked out My bay windows yet. I am still half asleep, My limbs are aching, and I am writing My secret Diary while lying here in bed. I am sure everything went well, though. I just hope the Board of Directors will never find out that it was I who created Eve. I would prefer everyone to believe she evolved naturally (if rather abruptly).

I am very happy for Adam that things turned out okay for him.

It makes Me kind of sad, though, to realize that, while Adam – the man made in My image – now has a partner, I am still alone, with no one to fetch My slippers, or make Me a cup of coffee, or bring Me breakfast in bed, or just generally look happy to see Me every time I return home after a day's (or a night's) work!

Maybe it is time I got Myself a puppy, or something.

7

Paradise
Redecorated

Dᴇᴀʀ ᴅɪᴀʀʏ,

Everything has been solved! There are no more problems in Heaven or on Earth!

I'm not sure how much this has to do with the arrival on the scene of the woman Eve. More than We can ever suspect, I imagine. Not only has she turned Adam's life upside down, she has been the source, directly or indirectly, of most of the changes that have taken place.

Poor Adam. At first, I felt almost sorry for him. Eve decided to redecorate the Garden of Eden, and Adam had to do all the hard work while she just stood there, planning all the new additions. And then changing her mind, so that he had to do it all again. And changing her mind yet again, back the way it was first time around. In the end, however, things got done, and peace descended upon the Garden of Eden.

Peace, and the chortling of little children.

Yes, the Adam's family has multiplied, almost immediately. They have two small boys now. They are called Cain and Abel. One is always playing with dolls (he will probably end up gay – but that is fine with Me, for I am a God of love and not prejudiced in any way), while the other is forever fooling around with matches and sharp objects. Eve is always watching over them to keep them safe from accidents.

And the Garden of Eden! What an astonishingly pretty place it has become!

There are little pathways and flower beds. There are lawns and gazebos. There are nooks and crannies and secluded spots where you can sit down on benches beside babbling brooks to relax or meditate or read a book. The animals are all well behaved and they happily line up for their monthly injections.

Eve has been so kind as to give Me a small puppy (how did she know I wanted one? It must be female intuition). It sleeps with Me at night, and goes for walks with Me every day at sundown. It is called "Dog" (which is, of course, an anagram for "God", in case you hadn't noticed – clever, eh?).

My own lifestyle has also undergone vast changes. Not only has the arrival of intelligent life on Earth altered My routine – I spend a lot of time there now – but I have also noticed a new atmosphere around here. People treat Me differently now. There hasn't been any talk of Board of Directors meetings or anything unpleasant for ages. Everyone in Heaven is very impressed with the success of the human experiment. Even the fallen angels down in the basement have been quiet of late.

Paul is the only bad-tempered person around, though luckily I don't see a lot of him. I expect he is secretly sulking. He is always expecting the worst, that chap. Can you believe it, he is still doing deals with Nietzsche (the Devil's lawyer), though no one even knows where the Devil is!

It was at Paul's insistence that Adam planted a lemon tree right in the middle of the Garden, and put a painted sign right next to it that says "EATING OF LEMONS STRICTLY PROHIBITED". Should Adam or any of his family ever eat one of these lemons, so the deal goes, it will be on record that mankind has chosen to serve the Devil instead of Me.

He explained it as a way of levelling the playing field. Something to do with free will.

I see no danger of that happening, though; lemons taste terrible, everyone knows that! Besides, there is a lot of other edible fruit all over the Garden, and Adam himself has promised Me that nothing of the sort will ever happen. So the problem of Good versus Evil seems finally to have been resolved satisfactorily. Eventually, if the Devil doesn't return, I might even consider giving the fallen angels down in Hell time off for good behaviour.

In the absence of pressing legal matters, and with no forthcoming general election to plan for, and precious little work that needs to be done – even the ghostwriting on My so-called autobiography has slowed down to almost a complete standstill – I have more time for Myself than I have had in millennia.

I spend a lot of time just playing with Dog, or going for walks through the Milky Way and its surrounding galaxies. Who would have thought that that insignificant corner of the Universe would one day become such a hub of activity and culture?

I have also started doing t'ai chi again.

There is, of course, always a bit of administrative work – the angels doing refuse-collecting on Thursdays must be given their rosters, there are roll-calls for band practices, and so on and so forth – but – surprise, surprise! – I have a secretary now who does all that for Me. Her name is Mary.

She was introduced to Me by, of all people, Paul!

When I said to Paul, "I thought you hated all women?" he just replied: "True enough, but Mary isn't an ordinary woman, she's a virgin."

"Oh, well, I won't hold that against her," I said, smiling mercifully.

And I didn't. Since she is very meticulous and also good with shorthand, I gave her the job right away. Of course, I won't pry into her personal life. As far as I'm concerned, she can remain a virgin for as long as she likes, so long as it doesn't interfere with her work.

A long era of peace and prosperity is beckoning for Heaven and Earth. I have finally got rid of all the negative influences and emotional baggage of My previous existence. My latest and greatest creative project, the Universe, is without a doubt a resounding success. Everyone agrees that though there may be other Gods around, and though They are all quite glorious in Their own way, I am the Most Important, the Cutting Edge, the Cat's Whiskers, the All-Knowing, All-Mighty, All-Powerful Leader of the Self-Catering Universe As We Know It.

Thank you, dear Diary, for allowing Me to pour My heart out to you during My times of crisis. I will continue to faithfully record all My doings now that things have quietened down a bit.

Part Two

THE
TURBULENT
YEARS

8

Paradise Lost

And then, one day, dear Diary, calamity struck, and everything I'd worked for was destroyed in one fell swoop.

I was on My patio, sipping iced tea and playing chess against Confucius, My new opponent, when I heard the news. It was My secretary, Mary, who came running, cheeks aflush, shouting, "God! God! You must come immediately!" She had My cordless phone in her hand. "It's Joseph, with an urgent message from the security company. An alarm has gone off in the Garden of Eden!"

"An alarm in Eden? Hardly likely," I mused. But I took the phone from her, and held it to My ear. Joseph was My new handyman and groundskeeper. "What's the story, Joseph?" I said. "This had better be good. I am about to put old Confucius here in checkmate!"

"I dunno, Master. It's that tree they're not suppos'd to eat from Y'know? Paul told me the other day to have it rigged. So that no cheatin' could take place. 'Course, the Adam's family didn't know about the alarm system. But it's definitely them that ate those lemons. I got 'em trapped real well on closed-circuit video."

A chill took hold of Me. If the crime was recorded on video, there was no way I could disprove it in front of the Board of Directors. And to destroy the video would be ethically indefensible. Creating a woman is one matter, but manipulating evidence isn't the kind of thing a God like Me should be doing.

"What exactly does the video recording show, Joseph?"

"It shows Adam and Eve gettin' pissed on a bottle o' somethin', Master, and climbin' into the tree with a knife to cut off some lemons an' squeeze 'em an' suck 'em dry. A real raucous party, an' just the two o' them, all naked an' laughin'."

"Didn't the video show anyone else? Are you sure?"

"There wuz … um … nope, nobody, Master. Well, no one human, that is."

"And animals?"

"Nuttin'. 'Cept for the snake curled around the tree. Asleep."

"Snake?"

There aren't supposed to be any snakes on Earth any more. They were the lowest form of dinosaur, and they were wiped out by that asteroid. Unless …

My brain was working overtime. There was a snatch of memory, a faint whiff of recognition teasing My mind.

Then, suddenly, it hit Me. The full truth. "Damn it!" I shouted, banging My fist on the table and scattering the chess pieces. Confucius went down on his hands and knees and started picking them up with endless patience.

"That night in the Garden …" I spoke in a barely audible whisper. "When I created Eve …"

"Been meddling again, have You?" Confucius asked, looking up with an amused expression on his wizened old face, but I ignored him.

"That hissing I heard in the undergrowth! I ... I think I know who it was."

I chucked the cordless phone to one side, stormed past the ashen-faced Mary, and strode into My study, where I kicked the sleeping Dog out of the way and opened the concealed door to My private liquor cabinet.

I stood there for several seconds, seeing the gap where the missing bottle had stood ... the telltale ring in the dust. And I knew there was only one other person in Heaven, Hell or on Earth who knew exactly where I kept My tequila.

∾   ∾   ∾

That was it, then. The beginning of the end of the longest period of peace and prosperity Heaven and Earth had ever known.

Everything went downhill after that. Paradise was closed down, and the Adamses scattered all over the planet. I eventually lost contact with them, and after a while, to tell you the truth, I lost My enthusiasm for Earth altogether. All the humans were interested in was drunkenness, debauchery and disorder. Last thing I heard, Cain had killed Abel and joined a rock group, Adam and Eve had got divorced, and pubs were allowed to remain open till after eleven. It was all very sad.

Worst of all were the things that happened to Me. As you can imagine, My reputation is in tatters. There have been leading articles in newspapers all over the Universe lately with headlines saying things like "GOD AT THE CROSSROADS", "LEADERSHIP CRISIS IN HEAVEN" and "WILL HE STAY ON FOR ANOTHER TERM?" The cover of the latest *Space-Time Magazine* shows a photograph of My face, close up, with a sullen expression, unshaven, and with all the grey in My beard showing.

And you know what? I'm not sure if I even care.

After all, I have My memories. And I still have Dog. And I still have some framed portraits of Me standing next to Adam and Eve. And I have My few faithful confidants and friends, such as Mary, Confucius and Paul.

Paul? Well, I must admit he surprised Me. Instead of saying "I told You so," or carrying on about legal matters, he has been very understanding indeed. He even bought Me a new bottle of tequila. You have to know Paul to understand what an unusual thing this is for him to do.

There are, fortunately, no Board of Directors meetings these days, but there are worrying developments downstairs. The Devil, according to rumours, has shed his snake disguise and returned from Earth, and has set up permanent residence in Hell. Apparently, he is very busy down there, building new wings, installing air-conditioning, and even setting up guerrilla training camps. On a quiet day, I can hear the sound of marching feet and triumphant yodelling down there. There is never any peace in Heaven with all their shouting and carrying on. Even at night, once they've finished playing rock 'n roll on their electric guitars, they turn on their TV sets very loud, probably to irritate Me.

But I hardly even notice them! I refuse to give them any thought! I am God, and they are just a bunch of twits! They are no better than the humans!

When I heard the news the other day that the whole of Earth was threatened by a high-pressure weather system which could cause a major flood disaster, I didn't even blink.

"Serves them right," I thought.

I do not care about the animals, either. Since they stopped receiving their injections, they have become quite violent once more. Even worse, there are more insects than ever before, especially flies. Though small, these creatures are every bit as revolting as the dinosaurs.

"Are You absolutely sure You don't want to convene a Board of Directors meeting to try to save life on Earth?" Paul asked Me only last week. "The situation can still be reversed, You know."

"I am quite sure," I replied. "In fact, I think I might just sit up all night and watch the flood through My bay windows."

That, at least, is what I intended to do …

9

The Flood

Howevער, the night Earth was supposed to be flooded, instead of sitting at My bay windows as I had intended, I found Myself slouching at My desk with Dog on My lap, sipping a tumbler of tequila and staring at the portrait of Adam and Eve in the Garden of Eden. And, before long, dear Diary, I was bawling My heart out.

I wasn't exactly drunk – being God, I can handle liquor exceptionally well – but I felt extremely tired and emotional, not to mention sentimental.

"Is this really the end?" I kept on sniffing to Myself, holding the portrait at arm's length to see better. "Will I never, ever go for a walk on Earth again? Will I never smell the flowers and see the trees and hear the waves lapping on the beaches again?"

When the emotion got too much for Me to handle all by Myself, I buzzed for My secretary.

She arrived, twenty minutes later, in a dressing gown and slippers, with her hair in curlers. She was obviously shocked to see Me in such a state. So was I (to see what she actually looked like when off-duty).

"Mary." I tried to keep My voice as business-like as possible. "I'd like you to run a computer search for Me. I want you to try to locate one upright man on Earth. If there is one."

She adjusted her hair, and stammered: "What's an upright man, God?"

"A good man. That's what I mean. Or, failing that, one who is separate from the rest of the human race. A recluse." I could see the incomprehension on her face. "Anyone who lives alone, or only with his wife and close family, far away from other people."

"I'll do that right away, God."

"Oh, Mary, and one more thing. Find out the current time ratio difference between Heaven and Earth."

She understood that. Mary may be a blonde, and a virgin at that, but give her an equation problem and she'll be on top of it in a jiffy.

She got back to Me barely half an hour later.

"The time ratio difference is three hundred and fifty thousand four hundred to one, God, in other words about forty years per hour. That means that, in Heaven, almost exactly a thousand years on Earth goes by in one day."

"Great!" I said. "That gives Me enough time. And the other thing you had to find out?"

"God, this one was a bit of a problem. The computer couldn't find a single good man on Earth. After I checked the men, I also checked the women, but no names came up."

"I was afraid so," I sighed. "Once they started sinning, they simply couldn't stop. And now the entire batch is rotten." I looked at the portrait of Adam and Eve again. "And all because of one lemon tree!"

"There is, however, one reclusive person. He is called Noah, and he lives all alone with his family on the shores of the Black Sea."

"Mmm," I said. "Is he unpopular? Why does he live alone?"

"The computer doesn't say, God."

I thought about this for a moment. Then I said, "That is it for tonight, thank you, Mary."

After Mary had left, it took Me only a minute to put on My raincoat, set Dog at ease with a bone from the fridge and a saucer of fresh water, and go to Earth.

I avoided the cities and crowded places, the boulevards where the prostitutes sold their bodies and insurance salesmen sold "Lasting Dignity" plans; I avoided the flea markets and orgies and pyramid schemes and the talk shows and the soccer violence and the riots and protest marches and false prophets and Tupperware parties and all the noisy exhibitionism of pre-Flood Earth society, and went straight to Noah's house on the outskirts of a gigantic forest on the shores of the Black Sea.

When I arrived, he was sitting all alone on his front porch with a jug of sangria and a joint, staring out across the sordid waters.

I appeared before him, as usual, in a cloud of fire, brimstone and assorted special effects.

"Whew!" he said, looking down admiringly at the joint in his hand. "This stuff is really good!"

"I am not a hallucination," I said in a deep voice to get his undivided attention. "I am God."

"Far out!"

"I believe you are Noah," I continued.

"Sure thing!"

"Noah," I asked, "why do you and your family live so far from the other people?"

"Because," he said, grimacing, "I practise a very unpopular trade. Everyone hates me."

"What are you, a politician? A lawyer? A serial killer? A rugby referee?" The more I spoke, the more high-pitched My voice became.

I could not help Myself; instead of Me getting his undivided attention, this man had *My* undivided attention. He was the most laid-back human being I had ever come across.

"No," he replied sadly. "I'm a builder."

There was a short silence. I got the impression he wanted to allow some time for the full horror of his statement to sink in.

Then he continued, in a mournful voice: "I've always been unpopular. Whenever a house I'd built fell apart, people blamed me. Whenever anything at all went wrong, they blamed it on me. Since it's started raining, things are so much worse, as You can imagine, for now it's not just broken taps and cracked walls and the usual complaints; it's the damp. The damp has seeped in everywhere. But how was I to know in advance of these changes in the weather? Everything is always against me. It's not my fault about cheap labour and high interest rates!"

"So that's why you moved out here," I said.

"Yep. I figured I'd rather be broke and unemployed out here in the middle of nowhere than getting sued left, right and centre in the city."

"Noah," I announced. "Do you have a pen? Do you mind taking down some notes? I think I may have a job for you ..."

"As long as You pay me up front and are prepared to wait a couple of months, believing that I am working mysteriously on Your behalf, though You cannot actually see any visible progress," he said.

"Noah," I said, rising to My full height. "This job is not for Me. It is for you."

When I returned to Heaven, I polished off the last of the tequila Paul had bought Me, and got even more tired and sentimental. I actually ended up getting My old guitar out of My wardrobe and composing a song on it. The song was an ode to the destruction of the dinosaurs and the humans.

The chorus went something like this:

I've seen fire and I've seen rain
I've seen sunny days that I thought would never end
I've got a lawyer but I still don't have a friend
And I really hope the dinosaurs don't ever come back again ...

I played the song to Paul the next day, but he was unimpressed. He said it wasn't even original! Can you believe it!

Mary liked it, though.

I am starting to like Mary. She is a bit dull, but she has a heart full of compassion and a good head for figures.

In the meantime, I am not sure how things on Earth have turned out. I haven't looked yet. Have Noah and his family survived? Did he remember to take two of every animal species (except the snakes and the flies) into his boat?

It doesn't really matter either way, I suppose. Even if the human race survives, the next batch will probably be as bad as the first, if not worse.

10

My First
Identity Crisis

Dear me,

I don't know why I still bother to carry on with this Diary. I honestly don't.

This is certainly not the official version of events – it's the simple truth. That is precisely why, if discovered, it could do irreparable damage to My career.

Ever since it has become common knowledge that a small group of humans, led by a stoned drunkard called Noah, had miraculously survived the Flood – and even had the astonishing presence of mind to save most of the animal species along with them, except the unicorns, hippogriffs and fauns – I have regained some respect and standing in Heaven.

But has this helped anyone? Has it made anyone happy? Has it turned the human race into nice people? They may have survived, but they are still a bunch of twits. More than this, they have become a pawn in a celestial game, and they don't even know it!

How could they? They are too busy satisfying their own twisted urges even to care. The latest news is that a lot of them have been trying to build a tower which was supposed to reach the sky. Fortunately, they started arguing before they finished, and now they have scattered all over the planet, developing different languages and cultures, the one as ugly and barbaric as the other. One group, who call themselves the Incas, practise human sacrifice and idolatry. Another bunch, the Egyptians, worship giant cats and do vast amounts of fornicating among the shallow reeds of the River Nile. The Babylonians are trying to make as much money as they possibly can. And down in Africa, where most of Noah's descendants went after landing their little boat on top of Kilimanjaro, everyone is too stoned and drunk all the time to be of any use to anyone.

What a series of calamities! What a comedy of errors! I am surprised so many folk up here find these humans so terribly interesting. I am embarrassed that I am credited with creating them. It is all a terrible misunderstanding. I should never have appeared to Noah. That was surely the last time, anyway. I have sworn a secret oath to Myself that I will never interfere in the affairs of human beings again.

However, even that decision has not brought Me peace of mind, for I am under tremendous pressure up here! Everyone is tense, everyone is competitive! The office politics is becoming horrendously complicated!

Paul reckons that, as things stand now, I'm assured of winning a general election. Even if you add up the Devil and his fallen angels, and all the bad people on Earth, who will most likely side with them, there are more than enough angels in Heaven to give Me the majority.

But the Devil's people keep delaying the election date. No one really understands their tactic. The population of Earth isn't increasing all that quickly – people are killing one another off almost as fast as they are procreating – so they won't get many more votes there. Some analysts believe the number of angels in Hell is swelling, but no one knows exactly how that is possible, since there have been no more dissenters from Our side. I know this, because Joseph, My handyman, has tapped everybody's phones so that he can report the first sign of rebellion amongst the angels who haven't fallen yet.

As if this threat isn't enough, there is the problem of this frigging book they are writing about Me.

What a travesty! It is, thank Heaven, no longer an autobiography, since I refuse to put My name down as the Author. But do you think that has stopped them? No, sir! Not only are they carrying on with their plans of publishing it, they seem to think that I am secretly pleased with it, that only a sense of false modesty is making Me act as if I am not interested.

All the facts have been distorted, obviously to flatter Me. As I mentioned before, Earth was supposedly created in seven days. The lemon tree in the Garden of Eden is no longer a simple lemon tree, but "the Tree of the Knowledge of Good and Evil". There is even supposed to be a "Tree of Life" somewhere. And – wait for this – the rainbow that appeared in the skies after the Flood was no ordinary rainbow; it was a covenant between Myself and mankind! As if I would even *think* of speaking to them again!

Why are they trying to squeeze kitsch little "moral lessons" out of these tragic and random events? Why are they trying to turn the whole sordid story into a Grand Unfolding Divine Plan? There is no such thing, believe Me! And I should know, for I am God!

It is all terribly depressing. And that is why I am keeping this secret Diary. I do it for the same reason that I go for a walk with Dog every afternoon at sunset. It is the same reason why I still keep the portrait of Adam and Eve on My desk.

It is My only peace of mind – the knowledge that at least I am honest with Myself.

I shall not let the good things go. I shall not allow the good memories and the simple pleasures of life to be overwhelmed by My duties as the Public Figure, Great Big Mr God, Boss of the Universe, Cult Personality, How Great Thou Art, and all that holy claptrap.

Thank you, dear Diary, for listening.

11
I Feel Sorry for the Jews

A<small>LAS,</small>

No sooner had I made that promise to Myself – the one where I swore that I would never meddle in the affairs of human beings again – when something very strange happened.

I fell in love.

Gosh, this is a long story, and I'm not sure where to begin. Let Me start by explaining, before I tell you the story, that the object of My infatuation is not a woman. Nor is it a virgin – for instance, My secretary. Nor is it My Dog. In fact, it is nothing that anyone would expect.

It is a nation.

Remember I mentioned the Incas, and the Babylonians, and the Egyptians? Well, these are all big nations, mighty nations, which rule over different parts of Earth at present.

But there is another nation, a nation rich in numbers but poor in wealth and power. They have no country they can call their own. Through some unlucky twist of fate, they have become the slaves of a stronger nation.

These people are the Jews. And they work for the Egyptians.

They have to carry and drag large stone blocks for hundreds of miles across the desert and then stack them on top of one another to build pyramids and stuff. For this, they receive no pay, and only the most meagre food rations. They sleep in squatter camps on the outskirts of the big Egyptian cities, and have to commute to work early in the morning in overcrowded caravans.

Not only are they financially poor, they are also culturally poor. Unlike the other, stronger nations, they have no dominant symbolism, no flag, no national anthem, and no rugby or soccer team. They are just slaves. They have never thought of themselves as anything else but slaves. For as long as they can remember, their lives have consisted of pure suffering.

Now, I don't want to promote masochism as a philosophy, but one reason, I reckon, why the people of Earth have turned out so decadent is that they have it so easy. Take the people who live in Sodom and Gomorrah, for instance. The valley where they stay is so fertile that they hardly have to work for their daily living. No wonder everyone is screwing everyone else without any thought for the future! (Not that I condemn screwing as such.)

Or take the Incas. Have they ever had natural enemies? No! That's why everything they do revolves around entertainment and sports. Even their human sacrifice is a form of voyeurism.

They are despicable, really. All of them.

Except the Jews.

That's why I have fallen in love with the Jews. That's why I have decided to start meddling again. That's why, for the first time since Eve gave Me the puppy as a present, I have this tingling feeling in My gut that says: Who knows? Perhaps some of the humans might still amount to something. Perhaps somewhere, somehow, there is a group of human beings who would be interested in getting to know Me, to choose My side in the battle of Good versus Evil. And perhaps that group of people is the Jews.

Okay, okay, I might have some ulterior motives. There might be other reasons, besides sympathy and altruism, that made Me go looking for, and finding, a group of people such as them. But hear Me out. I bet that, under similar circumstances, you would have done the same.

It started like this. One day when I was playing chess with Confucius I was interrupted by Paul. He walked on to the porch where We were sitting, looking very stern, holding a computer print-out in his hand.

"What is it, Paul?" I asked, pretending to be grumpy when, in fact, I was glad for the interruption, for old Confucius was about to put Me in checkmate.

"I don't know what to make of this, God," he said, handing Me the printout.

"But, Paul, this is just a copy of Our angel roll-call." The list contained the names and addresses of all the angels in Heaven; in other words, those who had not gone to Hell.

"There is one name too many. I've only noticed it now. See that name near the top? Right between Abdiel and Adnachiel."

"Abel," I read. "Now why does that name ring a bell?"

"Oh, I know Abel," Confucius piped up in his squeaky old voice. "Nice young man. But he's not actually an angel."

"Not an angel?" I said.

"That's impossible," Paul added.

"He used to live on Earth," Confucius said. "He was the gay one."

"What's gay?" Paul asked, visibly uncomfortable.

"That's right," I said, ignoring Paul. "He is a son of Adam and Eve from their first marriage! I remember, he used to sacrifice Me burnt offerings and perform all sorts of nice little rituals on My behalf."

"What's gay?" Paul asked again.

"You know, I've always suspected this," said Confucius.

"Suspected what? That gay people go to Heaven?"

"No. That human beings are supposed to live forever. That even if they die on Earth, their souls make the journey here."

"Then why has only Abel ended up here? Where are all the others?"

At that moment, Our conversation was interrupted by loud cheering and yodelling from downstairs.

No one said anything. We knew. Another soul had just arrived in Hell, and this was their way of welcoming him.

The silence was broken by Paul, who gasped: "There's no way We will ever win an election now."

Then he turned to Me, and whispered: "What does this mean? Do We have to find more gay people?"

"No Paul," I said, "what We need to find are people who will support Me. What We need to do is canvass some votes!"

Of course, that's what changed My mind. Initially.

For the first time in weeks, I focused My attention on Earth again.

No matter how much I told Myself I didn't care if the Devil should win the election, it really bothered Me that he should do so on the strength of the voting power of millions of human souls who had chosen to join forces against Me.

It bothered Me, that of all the people who had lived on Earth so far, only one had ended up in Heaven.

It bothered Me that, at this moment, Adam and Eve were downstairs, probably guzzling down bottles of tequila with the Devil.

It bothered Me that, because of the low profile I had kept on Earth lately, there were millions of people who probably did not even know of My existence! Unbelievable!

I often discussed this with Confucius over chess.

"If only I could find one group of people on Earth who would listen to Me. And who would then go forth and multiply."

"Rules out the gays," he said thoughtfully. "Have You considered the Chinese?"

"Don't the Chinese worship Buddha or someone like that?"

"Oh, there are lots of religions in China. In fact, there are lots of religions all over the world. Take the Middle East, for instance. Not everyone is equally decadent over there. The ones who worship Baal are quite a wild lot, but there is also a strong conservative element who believe in a new God called Allah. You might consider a coalition with some of these Gods, You know. At least They're not the Devil."

"Under no circumstances!" I exclaimed. "There should be no Gods besides Me. It's bad enough to compete with the Devil and a couple of million newly hatched souls!"

"You might yet turn out to be quite a jealous God," Confucius said.

"Is that a bad thing?" I wondered.

But his expression remained impartial, inscrutable, as always.

The rest is history. It did not take Me long to recognize the Jews' potential as My chosen nation. I wanted to rescue them as soon as I saw them, as soon as I felt their pain. I felt a mystical connection with them. I wanted to become their Tribal Deity. It was something I had never tried before.

Tribal Deitydom seemed to work for Allah, Buddha and some of the others. I was ready to give it a go.

I shall introduce Myself to them in the following chapter.

12

I Feel
Even More Sorry
for the Jews

So, DEAR DIARY,

My infatuation with the Jews led to an entirely new career – I am now a Tribal God. Never say you can't teach an old God new tricks!

Invigorated and optimistic, I have started taking an interest, for the first time in millennia, in Heavenly matters of state and politics. I want to plan, to organize, to work behind the scenes; in short, to beat the Devil in any way I can.

First of all, I asked Mary to do another computer search. This time, not to find God-fearing men on Planet Earth – I knew that approach was useless – but to determine the roots of the Jewish people. I wanted to know where they'd come from in the first place, and, secondly, how the hell they had got themselves into such a mess. I also toyed with the idea of asking Paul, since he was so good at that sort of thing, to write down their history in such a way that it would appear as if I had chosen them as My people since the beginning of time.

"The very first Jew," Mary reported back promptly, "was a nomadic farmer called Abram."

"Let's call him Abra-HAM," I said. "That sounds more epic. More mysterious."

"It gets worse from there," Mary warned.

"Worse? What do you mean?"

"Abram – or Abra-HAM, as You call him – was a certified schizophrenic," she continued, reading from her printouts. "He heard voices all the time. At one stage, these voices ordered him to kill his own son, which he almost did."

"He ALMOST did," I said. "Aha! The man had the courage to fight his own demons. An admirable trait!"

"Abraham's grandson, Jacob, was a professional con man and sheep thief. He started out on his career of crime at a young age by forcing his brother Esau to eat a huge amount of lentil soup just before visiting their father on his deathbed. Esau farted so much that his father chased him away and left all his possessions to Jacob." Mary blushed ever so slightly as she read this part.

"Enterprising," I mused. "But We'll have to leave out the bit about the farting. It won't sound very dignified in an official history of the Jews. And after Jacob?"

"After that, the family was forced by drought to move to Egypt to find work. Once there, Jacob's son Joseph became a famous fortune-teller at the court of the Pharaoh."

"Mmmm." I had a strong urge to change the topic. "And now? Who seems to be the most important Jew around at the present time?"

"I've already checked that on the computer, God. It is a half-breed called Moses, who stutters and who is presently on the run from justice for the crime of killing an Arab."

"I don't like the idea of killing an Arab so much," I said. "And the half-breed thing could be a problem. We'll work out a story about him being discarded as a baby or something. As for the stuttering – that's no good at all! How is he going to make inflammatory speeches, inciting his people to war? How is he going to turn on the charm in situations of international protocol?"

"He has a brother, Aaron, who is a stand-up comedian," Mary suggested helpfully.

"Excellent!" I said. "I'll go looking for them right away. What's the weather like in Egypt today?"

"Hot," she answered, without consulting her computer.

This Mary girl – I have to say it, at the risk of bragging, I think I made the right choice when I employed her. She is getting better all the time ...

I had seen, and even met, some strange human beings in My time, but nothing had prepared Me for the shock I got when I first encountered Moses face to face.

The reverse was also true, I guess. I must have looked as strange to him as he did to Me, appearing, as accident would have it, in the middle of a bramble bush (which promptly burst into flames because of My special effects).

Moses was a large, obese man with wild, staring eyes and a hairstyle that resembled weeds.†

And he was black. Pitch-black.

"Wh-wh-who are You!" he blurted, dropping his handful of anti-Egyptian underground literature (I found out later that he was the editor of an anarchistic magazine called *Exodus*).

"I am ... I am ..." But I never finished My sentence, which was

---

† I found out later that this hairstyle was called "dreadlocks".

supposed to go like this: "I am surprised to see that you are a black man.†"

"*I am*? Wh-what sort of a name is th-that?" he demanded.

"Never mind," I sighed. "Listen, I want you to fetch your brother Aaron and go to the Pharaoh and tell him I say he must let My people go."

"Okay," he said. "We'll go right away. Aaron!!"

From the flap of a two-man tent a few yards away crawled a scrawny little black man, saying, "Yes, brother! Yes, yes, my brother!"

When Aaron came and stood next to him, Moses smiled shyly and said: "Th-this is my brother, but m-most of our fr-friends call him S-Sammy."

"Sammy?"

"Why, isn't it ob-obvious? He l-looks just like Sammy Davis J-Junior!"

"Who's Sammy Davis Junior?" I asked, mystified.

"Man! My brother! Yes, my brother!" Sammy, I mean Aaron, did a little dance around his big brother, slapping him on the back as he did so. Then, the little man turned his attention to Me. "Say, Dude," he said. "Have You heard the one about the Phoenician, the Babylonian and the Jew?"

Moses held on to his authority. "Pack us a knapsack, a c-couple of sandwiches, and a whole st-stack of *Exodus* magazines. We're off to see the Ph-Pharaoh!"

"Yippeeeee!" Sammy cartwheeled, and disappeared into the tent.

When he was out of earshot, Moses turned a shrewd eye towards Me and whispered in a low voice: "Y-you know, I've always had the f-feeling that some day, s-something like this w-would happen."

---

† Thinking back on this moment, I wonder why the fact that Moses was black bothered Me so much. Am I a racist? Surely it is impossible for a loving God to be a racist? Or is it?

That was that, then. My introductions were made.

It is the year 1446 BC. I have exactly three human souls on My side: one gay man in Heaven, and two black men on Earth. But I guess One has to start somewhere.

13

I Still Feel a Bit Sorry for the Jews, but Not Quite as Sorry as I Used to

GOOD GRIEF! What a bummer! What a trip! What a scorcher!

It is impossible to describe in words the horror, the sheer tedium, the futility and the ghastly failure of the last forty years!

Would you believe it! We've just spent forty years in a desert! And a very small desert at that! We just went round and round in circles! Nothing went right!

I'm not sure if I like the Jews any more!

Moses is dead. Sammyboy is dead. Everyone We left Egypt with is dead. Only their children have survived! I have left a young punk called Joshua in charge, and returned to Heaven.

Frankly, dear Diary, I don't feel like going into all the grimy, grisly details right now. A very short summary will suffice. I am too tired to write, anyway. I think I will concentrate on the things that happened in Heaven rather than on Earth. They were also quite unpleasant, but somehow easier to deal with.

∾　∾　∾

Here goes:

As soon as I got back to Heaven after meeting Moses and his brother for the first time, I invited Paul and Confucius to watch Moses' encounter with Pharaoh on My new widescreen TV, which I had specially asked Joseph to rig up for Me in My studio.

They arrived all glum and despondent, which took Me by surprise. When I asked them what was wrong, Paul said: "The Devil has found out about You picking a favourite nation. He is furious that You didn't discuss it with the Board of Directors first."

(At that point I still felt very upbeat. Little did I know! Little did I know!)

"Stuff the Board of Directors!" I said, switching on the TV and setting the co-ordinates. "Mary, get Us some drinks, will you? Scotch all round, fellas?"

"A mineral water for m— Oh, never mind, I'll have a Scotch," said Paul. "To tell the truth, I need one."

"So what else did old hornface have to say?" I asked. "Ah, look! We're just in time. See, they have just arrived at Pharaoh's palace. Moses has just bribed the doorman to let them in by giving him a free copy of *Exodus*!"

"Why do the Egyptians all walk with their hands pointing straight in front of them?" Mary asked, glancing at the TV while setting down the drinks tray.

"For the same reason you wear curlers at night," I laughed.

"Perhaps they are practising to be mummies," Confucius said, and this time everyone laughed, except Mary, who didn't catch the joke.

"Anyway," said Paul, taking a very small sip of his whisky, "this may mean nothing to You, but the Devil says he wants an election next Wednesday."

"Wednesday! That's less than a week from now!" Confucius exclaimed. It was the first time I had ever seen Confucius get worked up.

"In Heaven, it may be less than a week," I said smugly, refusing to show any sign of alarm, "but on Earth, it's thousands of years. Anything can still happen. Look, there's old Pharaoh. What a fat old fart he is!"

"And there's his harem," Paul gasped. "How disgusting!"

"Turn up the volume," Confucius said. "What are they saying?"

I turned up the volume. The next moment, Pharaoh's laughter filled the room. On the screen, his gigantic body convulsed with mirth.

"Unbelievable! Unbelievable!" We could hear him say. "You know, I've always had a feeling something like this would happen!"

I turned My attention to Moses and Aaron. They were standing in front of Pharaoh and his whole harem and all his court jesters, looking rather sheepish.

"The Jews … the Jews want to leave! At last! And to announce this great departure, this irrevocable goodbye, they send a stuttering oaf and a midget who can only tell corny jokes! An exodus, indeed!"

He slapped his beefy hand on his knee, leaned forward to poor Moses and Aaron, looked straight at them, and growled, suddenly angry. "Of course you can leave! In fact, I'm ordering you to leave! I'm sick and tired of the lot of you! I'll pay you to go! I'll give you jewellery! I'll give you camels! Just get out of my sight! I never want to see another Jew for as long as I live!"

"This seems like a bit of an anti-climax," I said, as We watched Moses and Aaron leaving Pharaoh to giggle over a complimentary copy of *Exodus*.

"It's definitely the worst case of anti-Semitism I have ever seen," murmured Confucius, shocked.

"This will never do for the biography," said Paul indignantly. "I'll have to reinvent this whole scene. I'll stretch it out with Pharaoh pleading with them to stay, and with You smiting him and his people with all sorts of plagues ..."

"We can work on that later," I said. "Right now, I have to be off!"

"Where to?" They turned to Me, surprised.

"I'm personally guiding the Jews through the desert," I announced. "I'll be their column of fire in the daytime and their pillar of smoke at night. Or is it the other way round?"

"Why, doesn't Moses have a map?"

"Where are You taking them, by the way?"

I later heard what had happened after I left. Paul and Confucius would have seen snatches of this on TV if they'd cared enough to follow Our journey through the desert, but they got distracted by the bottle of Scotch, and started a lengthy argument about the relative merits of astronomy and astrology.

An hour later, I reappeared in the room in a cloud of billowing smoke, shaking the desert dust off My clothes and reaching for the bottle of Scotch.

"You've been away an awfully long time!" Confucius remarked between fits of coughing. "Did something go wrong?"

"And You look like hell," Paul added. "What's that stuff sticking to Your beard? Dandruff? No! You've gone grey! Your hair, too! Goodness me, God, You've turned completely grey in one hour!"

"Never!" I fumed, sitting down and putting My tired feet up on the table in front of Me. "Never, never ever again do I try to guide a bunch of primitive, illiterate, lazy, good-for-nothing slaves through that desert, or any other desert!"

By this time, Confucius and Paul were sniggering. "Tell us all about it!" they chortled.

"I gave them manna, they demanded meat. I sent them meat, and they fought over it. I gave them two stone tablets with all the rules on how to be the chosen nation, and Moses dropped one and lost the other on the way down the mountain. They made themselves graven images. They were caught lying, and stealing, and taking short cuts through the dunes. They didn't listen to a thing I told them! NOT – A – THING!!!"

I paused for a moment, and then concluded: "And if I have to hear one more joke about a Phoenician, a Babylonian and a Jew ..."

"This kind of puts Pharaoh's performance into perspective," Confucius said.

"Why does everyone hate the Jews?" Paul asked.

"Mary!" Confucius shouted. "Another bottle of Scotch, please!"

That moment was the beginning of My second identity crisis.

14

My Second
Identity Crisis

Dear diary,

The experience with the Jews in the desert had left Me tired; more tired than I had ever been in My life.

Designing the entire cosmos, arranging the Big Bang, and creating all the zillions of species of flora and fauna on Earth and on other planets had been nothing compared to *this*. I was *physically* tired – like the night I had to dig a hole for Eve, but infinitely worse! Weary to the bone, so to speak. If I had been depressed during My previous identity crisis, it was nothing compared to the utter weariness of soul, the cold blackness I felt now.

Nothing had any meaning. I did not feel like doing anything. Gradually, I cut Myself off from the outside world. I stopped seeing Paul. I no longer played chess with Confucius. I saw Mary only at tea-times, when she brought Me muffins, which, more often than not, she took away again, untouched, after tea-time had passed.

More than ever before, Mary became My only link to the outside world. She answered My phone, she took My temperature when I felt ill, and she conveyed My wishes to My subjects. In fact, she was My only friend, My sole sounding board, and – sometimes, late at night, when sleepless horrors overtook My frail and ageing frame – she became My sweet comfort.

Please don't misconstrue this last sentence, dear Diary. Mary remained a virgin throughout this period. Our intimacy might have resembled the intimacy between a man and his wife, yet, being God, I am incapable of physical sex.

Did I *love* Mary as a husband loves his wife? Well, that's a difficult question. God is love, they say, but, during this spell of existentialist angst and Self-doubt, I'm not sure I knew what love was. Suffice it to say that, in the words of George Bernard Shaw (from his memorable play, *Pygmalion*[†]), "I grew accustomed to her face."

While weeks went by in Heaven, and centuries on Earth, I saw no one but Mary.[‡] And *mostly* only during tea-times.

Of course, the business of running Heaven and the Universe, all the arduous tasks of simply being God, did not completely stop. Though I stopped making personal appearances, commands were deftly issued by Mary. More and more tasks were delegated.

Officially, I was still the Tribal Deity of the Jews, and though My heart was no longer in this project, I was supposed to show an interest in them.

Believe it or not, they had actually managed to settle themselves in the Promised Land by now, where they were living like royalty: eating, drinking, making merry, fornicating and serving other Gods. So I decided to rule them by means of a political dictatorship, and gave

---

† Or is this quote from *My Fair Lady*, based on the play? I can't remember which.
‡ During this time, My depression was so bad that the Earth/Heaven time ratio was actually slowing down, causing time in Heaven to appear to go by much slower than usual. I only found out later that this was the cause of much gossip and speculation.

them a king (they had wanted one anyway, hadn't they?). I reasoned thus: it was useless to try to appeal to their consciences, but at least they would respect the rule of law.

But to no avail. I had not counted on the fact that the kings *themselves* may be corrupt. Not only were they into idolatry and fornication, they were continually at war with neighbouring states and with each other.

I would send a prophet to them now and then, and sometimes they would listen for a little while before going back to their old ways. This happened over and over again. Occasionally I would arrange for them to be taken into captivity by some stronger nation, but they always managed to find their way back to Jerusalem – without any help from Me, mind you; makes one wonder why I even bothered to try to guide them through the desert in the first place!

I finally gave up on the Jews on the same day that My attention was drawn to a new crisis, a crisis closer to home, a crisis of such a deeply personal nature, something so utterly unprecedented, that I have difficulty talking about it, even here in the privacy of My own secret Diary ...

Part Three

THE
HIDDEN
YEARS

15
Something About Mary

D<small>EAR DIARY,</small>
   Mary is pregnant!

16
Another Very
Short Chapter

I MUST LEAVE HEAVEN immediately!

17

A Room
With a View

MISERY OF MISERIES! Scandal upon scandal!

Since My last entry, My situation has once again changed completely. I did not manage to make a secret getaway from Heaven, as I had planned. Well, I made a getaway, but not altogether secret. At least one person in Heaven knows where I am (Paul).

I am now an inmate! In an institution! I am being treated by a psychologist. His name is Dr Freud.

There is nothing to do here. Apart from My daily session with Dr Freud, I do a bit of exercise in the courtyard, some handcraft (mostly tedious tasks involving cardboard objects, raffia and lots of glue), and the rest of the time I spend in My room upstairs, staring out of the window and fidgeting with the sleeves of My institution-issued striped pyjamas.

This morning I received a letter from Paul. It did nothing to brighten My day. He has written to Me every day since I arrived here – these immensely long letters about faith, hope and love – and, if anything, they have made Me feel worse. I tossed this one straight into the waste paper basket after glancing at it and seeing that it contained the same philosophical ramblings and inane platitudes as all his previous letters.

Then I sat down at My upstairs window and stared out across the dreary landscape.

The institution is (somewhat euphemistically) called the 'Holiday Inn'. It was Paul who got Me a room here. It was Paul who told Me, when he caught Me trying to leave Heaven via a back entrance, dragging a large suitcase behind Me: "You are in no condition to travel. You need professional help."

I suppose I should feel grateful towards Paul. The moment I told him about Mary's condition, he leapt into action. She was medically examined. We looked at the sonar; it was established that she was expecting a little Boy.

Paul then sent Mary away discreetly. Joseph was ordered to accompany her to Earth, to help her through the birth, and to raise the Boy as their own. "This thing had better be kept under wraps," Paul said. "If *Space-Time Magazine* finds out what You and Your secretary have been up to, it will be the worst political scandal since Solomon ran off with all those concubines." I was too shocked and stressed out to protest My innocence or question his decision at the time.

Of course, the only thing I could think of was to hand in My resignation. But here, too, Paul's will prevailed. "All You need is rest," he said. "I know of just the place for You. It is called the Holiday Inn."

I suspected the truth right away. "I'm not going to any loony bin!"

"Not a loony bin, God. A Holiday Inn!"

"What's a Holiday Inn?" I asked suspiciously.

"It's a ... how shall I put it? A rest home for Celestial Entities. Bacchus has been there numerous times to sober up, so has Rastafari. The Dalai Lama practically *lives* there between incarnations ..."

"Who does the place belong to?"

"Oh, it's run by the Red Cross. They supply not only financial backing, but also a team of psychologists who provide personal attention. In-depth psychoanalysis of each patient ..."

So this is where I am residing at present (temporarily, of course!). I must admit, at least it is peaceful. Pity I couldn't bring Dog, though; no pets are allowed in the Holiday Inn. But I have My own private suite, where I receive VIP treatment: room service, sandwiches around the clock – in fact, everything but a minibar! (Apparently some other Holiday Inns provide minibars, but not this one.) According to the waiters here, I am the most high-profile patient the institution has ever had!

At the moment, there are only three other patients residing here (all of them struggling with problems that vary from premature deification to drug addiction): the Dalai Lama, who in spite of his great age resembles a six-year-old boy; a stern chap with a big white beard called Karl Marx, who is supposed to have something to do with politics; and Nietzsche, the Devil's lawyer (surprise, surprise!). I hardly ever see them. Especially Nietzsche, who keeps pretty much to himself (though I can hear him snivelling when I walk past his closed door).

So far, My sessions with Dr Freud have proved moderately helpful, if somewhat unsettling. Unsettling not only for Me, but also for him.

Yesterday, for instance, We came to a deadlock in Our therapy when he tried to question Me – of all things! – about My childhood.

What childhood?

I am God! I am a busy Person! I have never had time to have a *childhood*!

He appeared crestfallen when I informed him of this.

"But everyone has a childhood," he complained bitterly. "I have never met anyone who hasn't had a childhood. Especially not among my patients. Look at the Dalai Lama – he's had dozens! And You haven't had *one*! How do You explain this?"

"I was never born as a Baby," I explained. "I did not *begin* somewhere. I have existed since time immemorial. In other words, *at least*, say, nine and a half million trillion years. And even that is an arbitrary number! I may even be much older."

Upon which Dr Freud replied: "If You had no childhood, I cannot cure You. Everything that is wrong with anybody is the result of bad experiences before the age of two and a half."

"How about telling you I had a bad experience at the age of nine and a half million trillion years? What about *recent* bad experiences? Don't they count at all?"

"I'm afraid not."

Needless to say, the session ended rather abruptly. As I got up from the couch to leave, I could hear Dr Freud mutter German swear words into his thick beard.

Today's session did not go much better, when Dr Freud decided to question Me about what he calls My "God complex".

"Do You honestly consider Yourself to be the only legitimate God, the All-Powerful, All-Encompassing Being from which the Universe and all within it sprang?"

"Er ... yes."

"Then what are You doing here?" There was unmistakable hostility in his voice, and it made Me feel rather defensive.

"I am suffering from stress. I have had some troubles with lawyers. I have been betrayed by My friends. And, oh yes, My secretary got pregnant."

"Mmmm. Problems with Self-control, then?"

Dr Freud was a fine one to reprimand Me about Self-control, I thought bitterly. Him, with his office walls literally *covered* with faded black-and-white photographs of partially undressed women! The man has an obsession, that's for sure.

I should have been more sympathetic towards him and his problems. But, at the time, I was angry, and I snapped back at him: "No! It was an Immaculate Conception. I had nothing to do with it!"

"Yet You consider Yourself the Father," Dr Freud said cleverly.

I was stumped for a second. Then I thought of a good answer. "Well, metaphorically speaking, I am the Father of everything, all creatures great and small, all through the Universe."

"Including this illegitimate ... sorry, this *Immaculate* Offspring."

"Yes."

"And where is this little Baby now?"

"Last thing I heard, He was on Earth, living with a very nice family, and learning to be a carpenter."

Dr Freud must have felt a bit sorry for Me then, because he dropped his official psychological voice and started asking Me normal questions. "Have You ever considered a career change Yourself? Have You never yearned to leave behind all this high-profile political work to become a simple creative Person?"

"But, Doctor," I said, feeling that, at last, he was starting to pay attention to My real problems, "that's exactly what I was in the beginning. That's how it all started out. There were no politics back then. There wasn't even such a thing as Psychology. There was no need for it. I was alone. I worked with My hands."

"In other words, You were exactly like Your Son."

That statement gave Me a queer tingling sensation, as if I had heard it before, or knew it in another lifetime long ago.[†] I got up from the couch. "Do you mind if I leave now? I want to think about what you just said."

---

† I later found out that this feeling is called déjà vu.

This time he did not mutter German swear words into his beard as I left. He merely stared at Me, his eyes inscrutable behind his fogged-up glasses.

After the session I returned to My room, where I sat at the window for a very long time, staring out across the sloping lawns, the tennis courts, the flower beds, and the parking lot where the psychologists parked their luxury German cars.

Am I exactly like My Son?

I could not get that strange idea out of My head ...

Then, at that moment, Paul's latest letter was delivered to Me, and after chucking it into the waste paper basket, I returned to My now more familiar state of boredom and apathy.

18
My Third
Identity Crisis

H OWEVER, DR FREUD'S statement of the previous day had touched such a raw nerve that My feelings of bewilderment and confusion surfaced again this morning; and with them, an odd sense of sadness.

Today, before My session with Dr Freud, I sat alone in the court-yard, watching the Dalai Lama pluck the feathers from a chicken with his little hands (he was on kitchen duty), when I allowed Myself to think certain thoughts which I had hitherto suppressed very deeply.

Childhood. What exactly is it? Why is it so important? Humans experience it, all My creatures experience it in some way (except the angels, and Eve, but that could not be helped) – My *own Son* is experiencing it right now on Planet Earth – yet I know nothing about it.

For the first time, I'm starting to realize that, deep down, I have had mixed feelings all along about Paul's decision to send Mary to Earth with Joseph to give birth to little Jesus.

Though, superficially, I felt relief at the time because I had got rid of the immediate problem, another deeper part of Me experienced loss, and pain, and acute loneliness.

I realized today that the decision to allow Mary to leave had robbed Me of the opportunity to observe childhood at close quarters. It had, in effect, robbed Me of the joys of parenthood. If only I had been prepared to make the effort and take the time needed, I could have seen little Jesus grow up in front of Me, right there in Heaven.

Who knows? I could have trained Him to take over My job once it got too much for Me (it was already too much for Me).

If He proved talented, the pride of parenthood might have been enough to salvage My career *and* provide Him with a future.

In My mind's eye, I saw possible futures, different futures, futures which, because of Paul's decision, now lay forever beyond My grasp.

I could imagine large billboards spread throughout the Universe, advertising in bold print:

GOD & SON
Creative Design and Maintenance

This image brought tears to My eyes.

Not only was I sad, I was *curious.* What did little Jesus *look* like? So far, I had only seen the sonars, and they weren't very distinct. What did He sound like? What colour eyes did He have? Did He have any special gifts or aptitudes? Was He even vaguely aware of His lineage? What did He think of life on Earth? Was it as bad down there, from a human perspective, as it seemed from up here? What if Jesus grew up *enjoying* fornication and idolatry? What *was* it about these things that mankind found so irresistible?

What if My Son turned to a life of sin, and the media found out about it? What if He got to be stalked by the paparazzi from *Space-Time Magazine*?

As I sat in the courtyard, absent-mindedly watching the Dalai Lama working on his chicken, I was overcome by a sudden patriarchal jealousy and profound sense of ownership, and, all of a sudden, without planning to do anything of the sort, I let out a large roar, and shouted, for all the Universe to hear, in a voice so strong that the echoes of it would surely be heard even as far away as Earth (though some people might consider it to be the rumblings of a thunderstorm):

"THIS IS MY BELOVED SON! AND I REALLY LIKE HIM, YOU KNOW!"

For a few moments, I blacked out completely. It was as if My whole life flashed before Me, and I was looking at Myself from a distance. I realized, in that transparent instant, how many mistakes I had made, what a control freak I had been. I realized that the Jews would have been a happier nation if I had simply left them alone. I realized how bossy it was of Me to tell Samson how to wear his hair. I understood how My meddling with the dinosaurs had led to a chain reaction of unfortunate events. I understood that, once having created the Universe, I should have left it alone. That, because of My own foolish actions, I had landed Myself in a mess from which it was virtually impossible ever to extract Myself. And I realized that the first step to changing everything was to do nothing – to accept Myself, mistakes and all – and to forgive Myself. Only then could others truly forgive Me, and only then could I forgive them.

When I opened My eyes they were filled with tears and everything was blurry, but I imagined, for a moment, that I could hear and see the flutter of a giant flock of white birds stir up from a thicket of trees.

The next moment I came to My senses, and realized that what I had heard was the frantic flapping of the chicken. Miracle of miracles! It had sprung back to life, and with some of its feathers missing, whizzed several times around the courtyard before looping up into the air and out of sight.

The Dalai Lama let out a high-pitched yelp, and fell over backwards.

Nietzsche poked his head out through an upstairs window, looked at Me, and exclaimed: "God! What are *You* doing here? I thought You were dead!"

From the reading room in the western wing came the bellowing voice of Karl Marx. "What's all that racket? Has the revolution arrived?"

Dr Freud came storming out of the staff toilet, his hair and beard dishevelled, his trousers undone, and a collection of dirty photographs in his hand, saying in a trembling voice: "Did you hear that? Did you hear that? A primal scream!"

It was a Kodak moment.

I felt mighty relieved after that.

However, as any psychologist will tell you, a breakthrough in therapy is often followed by yet another low point. As Fate would have it, dear Diary, today's session with Dr Freud turned out to be the biggest shock of My life.

When I arrived at his office at the appointed time, great was My surprise to find all the patients gathered there. Instead of lying on couches, they were sitting in a semi-circle, on chairs.

Dr Freud was holding court in the centre, his brown suit crumpled and his beard all spiky and tousled. "Welcome to our first Group Session!" he beamed at Me hazily through a pair of spectacles more fogged up than usual. "Take a seat!" He gestured to an empty chair between the Dalai Lama and someone I had never seen before.

The other members of the Group were Nietzsche, who kept on looking at Me with a shocked, ashen-faced expression; Marx, who kept muttering from under his beard; and the unknown person, an enormously fat man with an even longer white beard than Marx's, a red suit, and rather laboured breathing. The longer I sat next to him, the closer I edged My chair to the Dalai Lama in order to get away from his irritating presence. My only consolation was that Nietzsche was stuck on the other side of him.

"Are we all here?" Dr Freud picked up a clipboard from his desk. "I have decided to have a Group Session because, in some way or other, every single one of our patients has had some kind of breakthrough today. This is your time to share these experiences with each other, and at the same time we will get to know our new patient ..." – he gestured at the fat man in the red outfit – "... who arrived today."

He looked around the circle expectantly. "Okay, who will start?"

The Dalai Lama cleared his throat. "Er ... you don't mind if I tell my story first?"

We all muttered in agreement.

"As you know," the Dalai Lama began, "I have lived on Earth, and will live there again, time and time again. Up till now, it has really bothered me that, though I have had so many childhoods, I have never been able to *enjoy* any of them. I have never owned a Dinky Toy. I have never watched a Noddy video. I have never even been to a house party, or got drunk with my mates! But today, as I was de-feathering a chicken in the courtyard, I heard a loud and booming noise, like a thunderclap, and all my lives flashed before me. All at once I realized that all life is suffering, and that everything I have endured has been for a very good cause, for the upliftment of all living things. My lives are all meaningful! Because of this realization, I consider myself cured, and I am prepared to face another incarnation, in which I will be much more dedicated and enthusiastic. I will start potty-training even earlier than usual. Oh, and I've decided to become a vegetarian."

There was a short silence. Then Dr Freud said, proudly, "What has happened here is that the Dalai Lama has reconciled his Id and his Superego." He looked at Us pointedly, then back at the Dalai Lama. "Very well, I will sign your release form tonight. You are cured. It's time to go back to Earth." He looked back at Us. "Next, please?"

"Er ..." It was Nietzsche who spoke next. "I have based my entire philosophy on the fact that God was dead." He glanced at Me accusingly. "Because I was so sure of that, I resigned as a lawyer and gave myself over to a life of pleasure and debauchery." He sighed. "Then, today, who shall I see sitting in the courtyard, uttering blood-curdling war cries?" He pointed at Me, spitting out the next word as if it were a venomous snake. "*God!*"

"Yes!" Marx boomed. "I've always said that God is a myth created by the ruling classes! Religion, you see, is the opium of the people!"

"Speaking of which," the Dalai Lama piped up, turning to Nietzsche, "maybe this shock was a good thing. Maybe you would have overdosed on cocaine otherwise."

"But I *liked* cocaine," Nietzsche moaned.

"Perhaps," Dr Freud said gently, trying to defuse the tense situation, "we should introduce our new guest." He glanced at his clipboard for the first time, frowning. "You are ...?"

The fat man in the red suit fidgeted uncomfortably, then announced in a gravelly voice: "My name is Santa Claus."

"And you are from ..." Dr Freud had trouble deciphering the information on his clipboard through his steamed-up glasses.

"From the North Pole. On Earth."

"Yes. Of course."

The fat man looked apologetically around the circle, his red cheeks blushing even redder with embarrassment. "I am here because of work-related stress."

"Ah, you see!" said Marx triumphantly. "The workers are alienated from the means of production!"

"I don't particularly like my job any more," said Nietzsche.

"Neither do I!" I said, speaking for the first time since entering the room.

"No!" Santa exclaimed. "I *love* my work. But that is exactly the problem. I'm only allowed to work once a year. The rest of the time, I have nothing to do but sort through my correspondence. I am bored – bored *stiff*. Besides, it is very cold on the North Pole."

"I've heard about you," the Dalai Lama said. "You are the guy who delivers presents to well-behaved children in the Western Hemisphere every December. To be perfectly honest, I didn't realize you actually existed. I thought you were a myth."

Marx frowned and fixed Me with an accusing stare. "Like I thought *that* guy was a myth."

"Hmpf," Nietzsche grunted.

"Oh, but I *am* a myth," said Santa Claus. "Wait, there is another word for it ..." He looked helplessly at Dr Freud, who instantly came to his assistance.

"The correct word you are looking for is *archetype*," the Doctor said. "The idea of archetypes was the brainchild of my colleague, Dr Jung."

"That's it," said Santa Claus. "I am an archetype. But that doesn't mean that I don't have feelings. It doesn't mean I don't get bored, or cold, or depressed. As long as the archetype exists in the hearts and minds of men, I exist. There is absolutely nothing I can do about it. I have no choice in the matter." He belched, and shifted his tremendous weight.

"Mmm," Dr Freud mused. "I wonder if archetypes have childhoods?"

"No, they don't," replied Santa Claus. "They sometimes have beginnings and endings, but they have no childhood."

The Dalai Lama stared at Me speculatively. "Maybe there are other archetypes besides Santa Claus," he suggested.

"Maybe some of them are here in this *room*," Marx said in a menacing voice.

All of a sudden, it felt as if everyone was looking at Me. The mist in Dr Freud's spectacles seemed to clear for a moment, and he said meaningfully, "Aha."

It was Nietzsche – trust him to give the knife a final twist! – who came right out and spoke the thought that had occurred to everyone else, including Myself. "I *knew* it," he said darkly. "You may look like God, You may speak like God, and yet You are a figment of mankind's imagination. Wow! Maybe I should write a book ..."

I tried to keep a straight face throughout this vicious exchange, but My mind was in a whirl. The implications of this notion were spinning through My head like balls on a snooker table.

What if this is indeed true? What if I never created mankind, but mankind created Me? What if the Universe would have existed whether I think I created it or not? What if I am merely fulfilling a certain wish? What if My very existence depended on imagery, literature, culture and conventions?

*What if I was in danger of becoming ... **obsolete?***

The only person in the room who was smiling was, of course, Santa Claus. There was a merry twinkle in his rheumy eyes as he nudged Me with his elbow and said: "Join the club."

19

The Globalization of Heaven and My Subsequent Retrenchment

NEEDLESS TO SAY, dear Diary,

I lost interest in the therapeutical process after that. Psychoanalysis had got Me more in touch with My own feelings, that much was true, but in the long run it was extremely bad for My Self-esteem. If I had carried on staying in the Holiday Inn, I would probably have ended up as a Very Self-Aware Non-Entity; a ridiculous contradiction in terms.

The next morning I packed My suitcase and said goodbye to Dr Freud.

"I was expecting You to leave today," he said brightly. "After all, You've had a primal scream experience, and You have made peace with the fact that You may not actually exist."

Though I felt like choking him with My bare hands, I just stood there, grinning like an idiot, while he pumped My hand and wished Me good luck. "So where are You off to now?"

"Back to Heaven, I suppose," I sighed. "I have some unfinished business there. And I miss My Dog."

"Well, I hope everything in Heaven is the way You expect it to be!"

he said. "If You ever have any problems adjusting in the outside Universe, just give us a call!"

I was about to turn and leave when he suddenly reached into his pocket and said, "Oh, I almost forgot! Santa Claus left You his card. He said if You ever felt like a holiday in the North Pole, at least You'll have his address."

"Hardly likely," I said, but I took the card anyway.

I left without saying goodbye to the other patients. They did not believe in My existence anyway, so I reasoned they would not see it as bad manners if I ignored them.

As I approached Heaven, though, I found to My dismay that things had changed a lot in My absence. There was a huge gate at the entrance, encrusted in pearls, and a thick, heavy boom barred entry. I tried to lift the boom, but it would not budge. I then tried to climb over it, but I had picked up too much weight from the full English breakfasts at the Holiday Inn to complete the manoeuvre. Only when I attempted to slide through underneath it, did someone emerge from a little guard booth.

"Halt! Who goes there?"

I crawled back from the cramped space, perspiring and embarrassed. "Who are you?" I asked as I got to My feet.

It was a fierce-looking man holding a large ledger. "I am St Peter, and it is my job to guard the entrance to Heaven. Name?"

"I am God," I announced, somewhat taken aback. "I am returning to Heaven after My stay at the Holiday Inn."

St Peter consulted the large ledger in his hands. He was frowning, and he wore spectacles (a more expensive-looking brand than the spectacles worn by Dr Freud, I noticed).

"And the surname is …?"

By this time, I was bristling with impatience. "I don't *have* a surname!" I exclaimed. "Do you realize Who you are talking to?"

"There is no mention here of any soul called 'God' who is allowed to enter," Peter explained, and turned the ledger around so that I could see the page he was on. Pointing with his finger, he said: "See for Yourself! The names on the list go straight from 'Galileo' to 'Goethe'. No 'God' in between."

"Surely there must be somebody here who will recognize Me," I insisted, tapping My knuckles on My large suitcase. "Call Gabriel! Call Paul! Call My Dog, for God's … um, for My sake! They will all vouch for Me!"

"I'm sorry, Sir, but we cannot allow nepotism here. If Your name's not on the list, then it's not on the list."

"And who compiled the list?"

"A guy called Calvin."

"This smacks of predestination."

"That's exactly what it is. Got any problem with that?"

I grabbed his shoulders and shook him. "Look, you can't go around deciding for people. Especially not in advance! That's the mistake I made with the Jews. Now I'm back from therapy and I want to correct those mistakes, but in the meantime Heaven has become more … more … more *regulated* … more *nouveau riche* than ever before! Look at all these pearls and precious stones! Where did you get the money for that?"

"You should see the streets inside," Peter said proudly, even though I was holding him by the scruff of his neck. "They've all been done up with gold paving. Very nice."

At that moment, to My immense relief, Paul appeared at Peter's side. He looked older than I remembered him, and he wore some kind of cape, embroidered with gold and silver. His bearing was sombre, his expression serious.

"Can I help You? What seems to be the problem here?" he asked in a grave voice.

I let go of Peter. "Am I glad to see you, Paul! Please tell this oaf that I am God and that I want to get back into Heaven. I need a shower and I miss the view from My bay windows and I'm mighty tired of all this bureaucratic claptrap."

"Oh, hello, God." He seemed to recognize Me at last, but greeted Me rather half-heartedly. "It's *Saint* Paul now. How was therapy?"

"Excellent, Paul, excellent, except for the last little bit, but never mind that. I feel much better, I am much more in touch with My inner Self, and I can't wait to get back to work! And what's with this 'Saint' business, anyway?"

Paul scratched his head. "The thing is, God …" He cleared his throat pompously. "As You have possibly gathered, there have been some changes here."

"That I can see. This whole place looks like Caesar's Palace."

"Indeed it is," Paul said. "We are working with Caesar now. We have opted for Earthly political power instead of the so-called moral high ground. It gives us more clout when dealing with the Enemy."

"And who is the Enemy now? Me?"

Paul averted his eyes, and continued: "No, the Devil is still the Enemy. But, in the light of Your recent track record, God, it has been decided that perhaps Heaven is better off without You. I mean, You were quite *cutting edge* in the beginning, designing the Universe and all that, but lately …"

"We *love* Your early work," Peter gesticulated.

"But You see, You stayed away so long ..."

"For a while, there were even rumours that You were dead ..."

"You never answered any of my letters ..."

"Then there is the rather delicate problem of stigma. You have been ... in an *asylum* ... You know ..."

"Not that it was Your own fault, of course ..."

"I mean, how reliable can such an ex-inmate be?"

"The bottom line is, God, You have become expendable. We have a new system going here, a very good system, even if I may say so myself, in which there is no room for You."

"You are a Has-Been."

"Yesterday's Hero."

"Retrenched."

"Though, of course, we will never forget You!"

"We still use Your name on all our letterheads ..."

As I stood there, listening to this barrage of betrayal and accusations, I felt Myself go completely cold, from the tip of My toes to the top of My head. It seemed, all of a sudden, as if My worst fears had come true all at once. All the darkest thoughts I had harboured from the beginning of time, all the guilty little doubts, all the wrong options I had ever considered (but never acted upon) ...

At that moment, a cock crowed in the distance. I thought of the Dalai Lama. Paul fidgeted with his golden buttons. Peter looked around guiltily. The atmosphere was thick with betrayal.

I breathed out, heavily. And I looked at Peter and Paul as levelly as I could.

I breathed in again, trying to work up the last vestiges of Self-esteem I had left.

Then I made a little speech.

Completely unrehearsed, of course. But now that I think back on it,

I suspect it was the best little speech I have ever made. Pity only Peter and Paul were there to hear Me. Had it been broadcast across the Universe, or printed in *Space-Time Magazine*, it might have represented My finest (if final) hour.

"This is never going to work," I said. "Earthly political power in a Heavenly context! Do You realize that We are all archetypes? No matter how much We wheel and deal, in the end Heaven, and everything in it, will exist only for as long as human beings, with some part of their hearts, believe in such a place.

"When they stop believing completely, Heaven will cease to be. What good will your political power be to you then?

"The Devil was right when he demanded a general election. For the destinies of all cosmic entities are indeed in the hands of mankind. They have the voting power, to them belongs the right to choose. They are the masters, not only of their own destiny, but also of Ours. No matter how crooked or corrupt they are, they are the only truly free beings in all of creation. It is true that they have abused that freedom. But nothing We tried to do could have changed that in any way. We acted like control freaks. We imagined that We were in charge of them. Vanity of vanities!

"You, Peter, you, Paul, I Myself, even Hell with all its demons and angels are mere figments of the imagination of the Universe. When the time is right, it will all cease to be.

"I am perfectly prepared to leave Heaven now, and never return, if that is the way you want it. But I have three demands.

"One. I won't stand as a Candidate in your general election. You can find someone else. I am through with politics. Even if you change your mind, I will not come back. Not only have you retrenched Me – I have simultaneously handed in My resignation. This parting of the ways is mutual. You will never see Me again.

"Two. I want to find out what's happened to My Son.

"Three. I want My Dog back.

"Thank you."

There was a long silence while the two men gazed at Me in a somewhat puzzled, appraising way. I could see that My speech had confused them – in fact, left them speechless.

But My victory lasted only for a moment. They were joined by a third person. It was a woman. I did not recognize her immediately. She was old, and grey, and slightly overweight.

"Hello, God," she said. "What's all this commotion?"

Then it dawned on Me who she was.

"Kathy Bates," I said. "I really *loved* your performance in *Misery*! Simply awesome."

"I'm Mary," she said.

I stared at her, just *stared* at her, for about five seconds (during this time, the first couple of decades of the Dark Ages passed on Earth).

"Mary," I repeated. There wasn't enough spittle in My mouth to say anything more than that. No explanations were possible. No words could convey the mixture of emotions I felt at that moment. The one line that could possibly have worked was "Love means never having to say you're sorry," and that actually occurred to Me, but, as I said, I didn't have enough spittle.

"Yes, it's me," she said. "Can I help You, God? As You see, I'm in charge of Heaven now. I have taken over Your old office and hung new curtains in the bay windows. You wouldn't have liked them anyway …"

I never trusted that woman, My mind told Me.

So that was the way the cookie had crumbled, then. She was the real power behind the throne.

The hierarchy in Heaven should have consisted of Myself, My Son and the Holy Ghost[†] – but We had been supplanted by Peter, Paul and Mary. A God-like trinity exchanged for a secular trinity, but still cashing in on the religious hype. Fascinating. Ingenious.

Sickening.

Mary looked at Me. "Jesus was here, but He didn't stick around. We don't actually know where He is right now." Then she turned to Paul, and spoke to him with an air of authority. "Paul. At least you can give the Guy His Dog."

Paul, in turn, looked at Peter, and the chain of command became clear. "Peter, tell God what happened to His Dog."

Peter was standing there, all embarrassed. He seemed almost truly empathetic when he looked up at Me and said: "We gave him away. I'm really sorry. Lucifer needed a guard dog to watch the gates of the Netherworld for him while he was away on business trips ..."

Suddenly, all My spittle returned. "You gave My Dog *away*?"

(And I couldn't help noticing, the Devil had become "Lucifer" again, and Hell was no longer referred to as Hell, but "the Netherworld" ... What was the Afterlife coming to?)

"Well, look at it this way, God. At least Your Dog has a job."

"Unlike You."

"Can't I just see him one more time?" I asked.

"You probably won't enjoy that, God."

"Er ... there's been some slight surgery done to make him look more vicious."

"Yes! But actually he looks quite nice! He's now got seven heads."

"Seven heads? I don't care!" I said, almost tearfully. "I just want to cuddle him once more."

"The thing is ..." Peter said. "He's also been brainwashed, I'm afraid. He now responds to a different name."

† The "Holy Ghost" represents My spiritual inner higher Self.

"What name?" I could not conceal the horror in My voice.
"Lassie."

That was the final straw. I turned away, and left. Would I ever see Heaven again?

Only later did I realize that, in My haste to get away, I had left My suitcase full of luggage at the Pearly Gates.

Oh, well. My suitcase contained mostly things I would never need again, anyway. Clothes that no longer fit Me. Some old photo albums (mostly of Adam, Eve and the children from their first marriage). A Christmas card from Confucius. Paul's first letters (I had kept the first ones, before I realized how boring they were).

I was better off without all that emotional baggage, anyway.

And I was certainly better off without a brainwashed seven-headed Dog called *Lassie*.

20
Both
Sides Now

O<small>H, DEAR DIARY!</small> What is the point of it all? Why am I still writing down My thoughts? If I don't exist anyway, My thoughts don't count! No one is interested in what I think, not even I Myself! I have been negated! I have been rendered non-existent! History has dumped Me on the dunghill of expired Symbols!

I have discovered, since My last entry (or pseudo-entry; since I don't actually exist, I am probably imagining that I am keeping this Diary!), that Santa Claus was right when he said that archetypes don't grow old and die. But neither do they simply cease to exist. I have found that out now. So Santa didn't know everything.

When their shelf life has passed, archetypes fade away, but they do not lose consciousness. They simply become *unemployed.*

To be unemployed is basically the same as not to exist. (Have you ever noticed that the unemployed masses are invisible to everyone else?)

Yes, even if everyone else has stopped noticing You, even if people walk right past You in the street without looking You in the eye, You still have feelings, awareness, a sense of Self.

Right now, the unemployment rate in the Universe has reached catastrophic proportions.

This is a fact; I read it recently in a copy of *Space-Time Magazine*, which I found lying about in a public toilet near Alpha Centauri. *Space-Time Magazine* has been publishing the unemployment figures of the Universe for aeons, and by their own admission the figures have never been as high as now.

"Never before in the history of civilization," they write, "have so many once powerful symbols lost their potency so fast. As mankind races into the third millennium, and as interest in the long-awaited general election is dwindling, more and more humans have opted for force rather than the democratic process. Not only are they discarding their Gods one after the other (at this point, only Allah and Santa Claus still have grassroots support, and Santa's followers tend to abandon him when they turn six or so); they are indeed heading for mass self-destruction by their own nuclear weapons. Of course, should this happen, every single archetype throughout the Universe will become redundant, and the unemployment rate, already sky-high, will rise to precisely 100%."

Of course, it is probably rather stupid of Me to look for work. I have had a long and illustrious career as God. I can retire if I want to – just enjoy My invisibility, go to some planet with a nice climate and sit in the sun. Grow My own vegetables. Read some books. Et cetera.

But I can't just go off and do that. To do such a thing would be to capitulate. To give up. I *need* to work. I have the urge to feel useful!

So I spend a lot of time hanging around employment agencies, filling in forms, and waiting for people to call Me back. Which, of course, they never do!

By now, I know the employment form by heart. It goes like this:

NAME:	God
AGE:	Approximately nine and a half million trillion years
RACE:	None
SEX:	None
MARITAL STATUS:	Single
RELIGIOUS PERSUASION:	Atheist
PREVIOUS OCCUPATION:	Created everything
REASONS FOR LEAVING PREVIOUS OCCUPATION:	Secretary got pregnant
OCCUPATION SOUGHT:	Anything
SPECIAL APTITUDES:	Arithmetic and a bit of quantum physics (and I have also written a song or two)
REFERENCES:	Dr Freud (Holiday Inn), Santa Claus (North Pole, Earth), a seven-headed dog called Lassie (Netherworld)

Being part of the unemployed masses has certainly been an eye-opener. The people I've met! The places I've seen! The horror! The horror!

While standing in queues in the dark and dingy corridors of countless employment agencies all over the Universe, I have got to know at close quarters, to name but a few:

A down-and-out fortune-teller named Nostradamus.

A very depressed ex-mathematician called Isaac Newton.

Attila the Hun.

Rupert the Bear.

Some other Gods, who used to be stiff competition for Me, but who were now equally down on Their luck, such as Zeus, Ra and Baal.

A guy who calls himself Sir Jeffrey Archer.

Dr Freud (yes, the very same Dr Freud; he told Me that the Holiday Inn had been taken over by a consortium that wanted to develop it into a chain of hotels. I had to change his address on My REFERENCES list after this unfortunate meeting).

Several philosophers, of whom by far the most eccentric one was a fellow called Descartes, who kept talking to himself, repeating the same statements ("I am. I think. I think. I am, I think. Therefore! Therefore! I am!") over and over again.

Nietzsche (yet again; will I never stop bumping into that idiot?).

Superman (alias Clark Kent).

A very unpleasant little Austrian called Adolf.

Rasputin.

A number of former Springbok rugby coaches.

A caped Boy Wonder called Robin (Batman didn't want him any more).

Dr Fritz Gaum (a magazine editor).

An entire pop group called the Village People.

Tarzan and Jane.

Homer Simpson.

The Lone Ranger.

Art Garfunkel.

A slithery creature called Gollum.

Karl Marx, who, much to My surprise, beamed an uncharacteristically bright smile at Me and informed Me that, since our last encounter, he had turned into a "born-again Christian" (whatever that is).

The Camel Man (who suffered from a bad cough).

A musician called Peter Frampton.

A cuddly little person in a tight-fitting woollen suit called Tinky-Winky.

Literally hundreds of Elvis impersonators (one of whom might have been Elvis himself, but it was impossible to tell).

And a guy wearing a diaper who claimed to have appeared on *The Jerry Springer Show* twice.

Of course, during all this time I kept My eyes and ears open for My Son, but information about Him was very scarce. The only facts I managed to gather were, sadly enough, on the Obituary pages of a very old *Space-Time Magazine*, where I tracked down a mysterious reference that went like this:

> *Deceased and Risen from the Dead (Rumoured to). Jesus Christ, only-begotten Son of former "God". Sadly missed by Mary Magdalen, Nicodemus, John and everyone else in first-century Israel (except the dickheads of Bethlehem). We still fondly remember Your last words, Jesus: "I'll be back!" Is that true, or should we expect another Messiah?*

I was not sure what to make of this. Was it a hoax? If not, was the Jesus referred to My Son, or was it an impersonator? What was all this talk about a "Messiah"?

More than once I toyed with the idea of going to Earth personally to look for clues of His whereabouts (I had not been there since the time the Jews had got themselves lost in the desert!). But a number of things put Me off this plan of action. Firstly, I had very bad memories of that place. Secondly, the levels of unemployment, violence and crime were worse there than anywhere else in the Universe. And, thirdly, there were millions of lawyers. This was a fact I'd heard from Nietzsche while We stood chatting in a queue in an employment agency somewhere west of Galaxy 98430952216X.

"I'd love to play Devil's advocate and encourage You to go to Earth, God, but the truth is, if the lawyers on Earth recognize You, they'll sue You till Kingdom come," he said, scratching his armpits (he was suffering from the advanced stages of some venereal disease).

"Sue Me? Why? What have I done to them?"

"You see, God, almost every legal document on Earth has a special clause that says you can't sue anybody for so-called 'acts of God'. This includes stuff like earthquakes, famine, bush fires or floods. The minute You set foot on Earth, and they get to hear about it, everyone will be after You to sue You for the damages they've incurred from every natural disaster throughout history! You'll be paying off debts till You're *fifty* million trillion years old."

This was a scary thought. If there was one thing that really frightened Me, it was lawyers, especially lawyers who could speak Latin. Nietzsche informed Me that all lawyers on Earth indeed spoke Latin very well, and often used it to intimidate their own clients.

Yet I was not convinced straight away. "But how will they recognize Me? I'm not that famous any more. Since becoming unemployed, My picture hasn't once appeared in *Space-Time Magazine*. Only four people have asked Me for My autograph recently, and of those, three apologized afterwards, saying they had confused Me with Demis Roussos."

"And the fourth?"

"The fourth was someone collecting signatures for a petition against cloning humans."

"Oh."

"So you see, it's probably safe to go. And, in any case, I'm looking for My Son, and I'm planning to go to Earth at Christmas time, because maybe I'll find some clues at His birthday celebrations."

It was the best plan I could come up with. In My investigations I had learned that Santa Claus – of all people! – was involved in the birthday celebrations, so maybe he could point Me in the right direction. And I had worked out that, with all the weight I had gained, his red outfit would just about fit Me by now.

If I were to return to Earth, I would feel safer wearing a disguise ...

Before going to Earth, I wrote a poem about how My status in the Universe had changed, from that of Supreme Creator to an unemployed Nobody, a Bum forgotten by everyone.

The poem went like this:[†]

I've looked at life from both sides now
From give and take, and still, somehow
It's poverty and unemployment I despise
I really don't understand private enterprise

I folded it up and put it in My pocket to show to Santa Claus. It was meant as a peace offering. I couldn't stand the guy, but I needed him, and if I showed him a poem I'd written, I reckoned he might just feel more obliged to help Me with My plan.

---

† I wish I could compose a tune for it, but My guitar is still in Heaven.

21
Countdown
to Armageddon

ENTERING EARTH'S ATMOSPHERE for the first time after such a long absence was a strangely alienating experience. Alienating in more senses than one – the stratosphere around the planet was literally crawling with alien space ships. This surprised Me, as I had not realized that other intelligent life forms had evolved in the Universe since I had lost My job. I wondered why they seemed so interested in Earth. Invisible to most human beings (except some Americans), these little doe-eyed creatures were engaged in drawing mysterious patterns in cornfields, scaring cattle, and performing strange operations on certain unlucky people.

When I asked them what their business was, they informed Me that they were just about to leave. "We are estate agents," they explained, "and we come from the other side of the Milky Way. We have been looking for suitable planets to expand our property market. But the political situation on Earth is so unstable right now that we have decided to pull out. The humans have just started their Third World War, and their ecology is on the verge of going bust."

"How come you are so far evolved if you started so long after the humans?" I asked them.

"Oh, but the humans were the first, remember?" they replied. "They were the prototype for everyone else. We've researched their history. It took them *millennia* to discover something as simple as fire. Then they *really* took their time designing the wheel. After that, nothing happened for what seemed like *forever*. While we carried on developing at a normal, consistent speed, they had a very slow start. Can You believe that they only found out about quantum physics *a few years ago*? And that's not all! The men in their species have built the most unbelievably high-tech weapons of mass destruction, but most of them are still unable to untie the clasp of a woman's bra with one hand in the dark."

"That's terrible!" I agreed, suddenly eager to conclude the conversation. "By the way, which side is the North Pole again?"

"That way," they said, pointing to the ice cap at the top. "Are You just visiting?"

"Yes," I said.

"Better keep it short," they advised. "Bye!"

I headed straight for Santa Claus's hideout. I had to be quick, not only because the world was about to end, but because it was only two weeks before Christmas, and I didn't want to miss him. Right now he'd probably be hard at work wrapping presents, servicing his sled, and so on.

When I arrived at the fat man's place I found everything in complete disarray. His reindeer were wandering around in a dazed state. The door to his house was wide open, and snow covered the threshold. Inside, I found his lounge littered with empty bottles. An ashtray was overflowing with cigarette butts. Santa himself was fast asleep next to a TV in a smelly little room at the back. Without his red outfit, he looked more unattractive than ever. He was snoring rather loudly.

The TV was on. I could see footage of missiles being readied to fire. A grey-haired President was making angry speeches, talking about war.

While I waited for Santa Claus to wake up, I rummaged around his house. Everything about the place had the feeling of a man at the end of his career. His files were in disorder. The cups in the kitchen were grimy. There were liquor stains on the carpets. The fridge was stacked with half-eaten cartons of Kentucky Fried Chicken. This was the house of a man who had given up on himself.

When he eventually woke up, he confirmed My worst suspicions.

Santa seemed glad to see Me, but he made it perfectly clear that he was at a low point in his life.

"I am ever so depressed, God," he said. "I was supposed to work tonight; it's almost Christmas Eve, and my paperwork and address lists need to be updated! Oh, well, with the world in the state it is, there are hardly any well-behaved children left anywhere. I blame it on Dr Spock. Since he became fashionable, I have had just about nothing to do. Anyway, at least the North Pole isn't quite as cold as it used to be. The Greenhouse Effect has helped to make things a bit more bearable around here. Would You like some coffee?"

"Thank you," I said, and then came straight to the point. "I'm looking for My own Son. You must know about Him. He died a long time ago, but He rose from the dead. I've heard you have something to do with His birthday celebrations. Can you help Me at all?"

"Never met Him," Santa replied. "Christmas might be named after Him, but my job is simply to give presents to children. Kids love me, and I make a tidy commission from the toy manufacturers."

While I drank a cup of coffee, he opened himself a bottle of Scotch.

"If You want to find out about Your Son, go look for Yourself. Ask around. I'm sure there are lots of folk who know much more about Him than I do."

"I'll need a disguise," I said. "Can I borrow your red outfit?"

"Oh, sure!" Santa replied. "But try to be back before Christmas Eve. I might have a few gifts to deliver after all. That is, if the bombs haven't wiped everyone out yet. I hope my reindeer aren't on strike. They have a trade union these days, can You believe it?"

"I don't need your reindeer," I explained. "I can get around on My own. I just don't want anyone to recognize Me."

"Well, You've picked the right time," Santa said, as he fetched Me his outfit. "There are lots of people wearing Santa Claus outfits right now. There's at least one of them in every shopping centre! If You can stop Yourself from changing water into wine or walking across puddles, no one will suspect that You are anything but a regular guy with a false beard and a red jacket."

He turned away and went back to his bedroom. I set out to see the world in My red outfit. It was a bit loose, but it worked. In fact, I caught reflections of Myself in the windows of buildings, and I quite liked what I saw. Idly, I wondered if Santa would let Me have his job once he decided to retire.

Seeing Earth from close-up for the first time in thousands of years was quite a shock! The first thing I noticed was how crowded it had become. Not only crowded, but also dirty. The streets were dirty, the sky was dirty, the sea was dirty, even the people seemed dirty. Sallow-skinned men and women moved around in a tremendous hurry on the pavements of the cities. Many of them looked like lawyers, with suits and briefcases, but I couldn't be certain. They seemed depressed and angry. They drove around in cars that emitted poisonous fumes. They were burning lots of things – in some places cattle, in others entire oil fields, in others piles of books. I wondered if these were meant as offerings to some new God.

After criss-crossing the Earth and pausing here and there to make inquiries, I still didn't know where My Son was. Santa had been right, however, when he said that everyone knew about Him. I even saw His name here and there on billboards. I gathered that, in the minds of Earth people, He had something to do with money or banking, because some of the billboards said "Jesus Saves". Possibly some kind of financial cult had sprang up around the memory of Him.

I visited Paris and checked out some paintings in the Louvre. I went to Jerusalem and was appalled to see that the Jews were still fighting with everyone. I had stones thrown at Me in Afghanistan (they probably didn't like My outfit). I drank some beer in Australia, went on a hiking trail in Peru, and went up the Table Mountain cable car in Cape Town. Everywhere I heard the same story: that Jesus had been on Earth and left again. That He had promised to come back, but never had. Most people felt that He was a bit unreliable. They doubted whether anyone would ever see Him again. I even managed to track down the head of the financial organization that apparently worshipped Jesus, a very old guy called the Pope who wore a cape and lived in Rome. He had Me thrown out of his office before I could ask him any questions.

It was true what *Space-Time Magazine* had claimed and what the aliens had warned Me against: Earth was in a terrible state, politically, socially and ecologically. There were floods, and droughts, and famines, and wars (little ones and big ones), and riots, and pestilence, and earthquakes, and plagues, and the most awful goings-on! The thing that I found most upsetting was the plight of the children who had to grow up in these circumstances. My heart bled for them. I wanted to hold them to My breast and tell them I loved them! I wanted to take over Santa's job and bring them gifts! They were so lonely, and so hurt, and so hungry, and so neglected, and the parents did not seem to care for them at all! And yet the parents went to war in the name of their children. I even heard people using My name in support of war. If I still had a lawyer I would have sued for defamation for sure.

I was thoroughly depressed. I was in a place called Disneyland, wandering around in a daze. The whole place was lit up with coloured lights and Christmas decorations! It was supposed to be My Son's birthday, but He was nowhere to be seen! The whole idea of Christmas was a farce! I had never felt so lonely in My life, not even when I was unemployed and hanging out in the most dismal and dingy corners of the Universe.

During this time, though I had been unable to find My Son, though I had in fact encountered nothing but fake memories and grossly distorted myths which obviously misrepresented the idea of Him, it gradually dawned on Me why He had never returned. The whole sad story – or a Baudelerized version of it – was told in the Gideon Bibles I encountered in every hotel room.† How Jesus had gone around curing the sick and driving out evil spirits and doing tricks with wine and sandwiches and generally being the life and soul of every party. How He had been crucified by the Romans. How He had risen from the dead (good for Him!), and gone to Heaven (where, as I knew now, He did not stay very long). And now He was gone for good. How could any sane Person, any run-of-the-mill Messiah, return to a planet where He had received such treatment?

I knew, instinctively, that, wherever He was, He was fine. That He was probably in therapy somewhere, and trying to put that whole

† My "official" biography, for which I have never received any royalties!

terrible sequence of misfortunes behind Him. And if humankind would just come to its senses, they would be fine too. I realized that the chances of this happening were very slim, but if it ever happened, the change of heart would begin with the children (whether they were well behaved or not). If this war failed to kill everyone, such a generation of conscious human beings may well arise to claim the Earth back as their own, minus all the war, pollution and stupidity. This would happen whether I meddled with them or not. Call it evolution. Call it whatever you want. Humanity did not need Me, neither did they need any other Gods. They only needed to notice, *really notice*, their own children.

One afternoon, as I was sitting nursing a beer in a badly lit bar in the red-light district in Amsterdam – don't ask Me what I was doing there! – I thought about My Son, and all the other children of the world.

Maybe it was the alcohol, maybe the stress of seeing so much trouble in the world, but I cried like a baby, putting My head on the bar counter and spilling the contents of My half-empty beer glass all over Santa's outfit. I wept for the hopelessness of human existence, for the loneliness and the pain and the courage and the hunger and the cold and the need, the physical needs that drove people to lives of crime and fear and misdirected passion. I wept for every human being that had ever walked the face of the Earth. I loved them all, I wanted to forgive them all everything they had ever done wrong. I wanted to tell them: "It's all right, I'm just as unhappy as you are, just as unemployed, just as broke. And this war, if it kills all of you, might just kill Me, too. And even if I do survive, I'm not sure that I'm prepared to go through all the trouble of designing this self-catering Universe, and all the stuff in it, ever again!"

I only woke up hours later because someone was shaking Me by the shoulders.

As I looked up from the puddle of spilt beer and scattered nuts I had been lying in, there was Mother Theresa.

As her face swam into focus, I realized it wasn't Mother Theresa at all. It was the old barmaid. "Wake up, Santa!" she laughed. "Don't You have work to do tonight?"

EPILOGUE

22
The Last TV Supper

AND SO, FINALLY, dear Diary,

I rushed back to old fatso's hideout. I was sure that he would be waiting impatiently for his suit, his sled loaded with presents and his reindeer ready to fly. Great was My surprise to find him even drunker than before, and his house in still greater disarray.

"You're drunk," I gasped.

"You're wet," was his retort.

"Yes. I knocked over a glass of beer. I'm sorry if some of it spilt on your costume."

"Oh, don't worry about that!" he belched. "Come in, come in. You are just in time – I have just ordered some Kentucky Fried Chicken."

I stood there, not knowing what to say, thinking with bewilderment of all the children who were going to miss out on gifts tonight because Santa was drunk.

Santa misinterpreted My reticence. "What, don't tell me You didn't know we had Mr Delivery in the North Pole? Do sit down, have some Scotch! Do You prefer wings or drumsticks?"

Since it was the festive season, I joined him in his Scotch-drinking. So there We sat, Santa and I, eating Kentucky Fried Chicken and drinking Scotch, Santa getting uproariously drunk and Me feeling more and more sentimental, while, on the TV screen, people were shown rioting and fighting in the cities of Earth. It was a bizarre situation. Since Santa still didn't have any clothes on, I first wanted to call this chapter in My Diary "The Last Naked Supper", but it sounded a bit too much like William S. Burroughs.

Speaking of literature, around midnight I remembered that I still wanted to show Santa the poem I had written. I was too sentimental to find it in My pocket, so I recited it to him.

He was visibly moved, though it might have been the Scotch talking. "It's a wonderful poem," he said. "I wish I could remember the tune."

"There isn't a tune," I replied. "I haven't composed the tune yet."

"Oh, but there is," he said. "I've heard it on the radio. It went like … it went like …"

I decided to change the topic. I raised the issue of whether his job was available.

"Oh, of course! You can move in here anytime. You can have my outfit! And my reindeer! I was about to retire anyway."

The offer surprised Me. "But I thought you loved your job!" I said.

"I used to," he nodded. "But things have changed. I …" He hesitated. "I don't know how to tell You this, God, but I have a confession to make. I have not exactly been straightforward with You up till now. I have a dark secret, a secret that I have kept from You since time immemorial."

"We have not known each other very long," I said, thinking that Our conversation was sounding more and more like a divine soap opera. "You have hardly had time to lie to Me."

"Oh, We have," he contradicted Me. "We have known each other a very, very long time indeed. The only reason You haven't recognized me is because I got so fat. Mind You, You Yourself have attained a fuller figure as well. But I have been following Your career very closely. In fact, I went to the Holiday Inn only to spy on You."

This totally confused Me. I stared at Santa blankly.

He continued: "I guess You might say I owe You an apology."

"The only person who owes Me an apology," I said, "is the Devil."

"You still don't get it, do You? What is my name? Do I have to spell it out for You?"

"Santa?"

On the TV screen, the first missile exploded. A mushroom cloud went up. Opposite the table from Me, I saw a very fat, very naked man with a chicken drumstick in one hand and a glass of Scotch in the other. He was grinning in a sad sort of way.

I stood up, aghast, as the full truth of what he was saying hit Me like a gust of icy arctic air.

"You ... you are Satan. *S – A – T – A – N.* The *Devil!*"

He nodded affirmatively.

"You ... beat Me," I gasped. "*Without a general election.*"

"I didn't need an election any more," Satan said. "It wouldn't have been free and fair anyway. There have been far too many irregularities. You sneaking off to create Eve in the middle of the night ... me stealing Your Dog ... Jesus dying for everybody's sins ... the Beatles splitting up at the worst possible moment ..." He sighed. "But You know the rules, God. *I haven't actually won.* At this point, it's still a draw."

He put down the glass heavily. "Things could still go either way." He looked at the TV. "It depends on whether there's anybody left after this war."

Another missile exploded. And another. It reminded Me of Guy Fawkes.

"You're a myth," I said. I was grasping at straws, and We both knew it. "You don't actually exist."

He had finished eating his drumstick and was fishing around in the carton of Kentucky Fried Chicken for something. Finally his hand emerged. He held something out to Me between his thumb and forefinger. It was a wishbone.

"The war is real," he said. "This wishbone is real."

I stuck out My hand, and grasped the other end of the wishbone between My thumb and forefinger.

"And," he said, "if I win this bet, my victory will be real."

For the first time in My nine and a half million trillion years of existence, I felt like praying. But there was nothing there.

No faith. No love. Only the faint, very faint glimmer of hope.